MURDER AND A PINCH OF ROSEMARY: THE DONAHUE BROTHERS OF TEXAS, BOOK 1

TEXAS-SIZED MYSTERIES, BOOK 3

MICHELLE FRANCIK

SWEET PROMISE PRESS
PO BOX 72
BRIGHTON, MI 48116

THE SCENT of peppermint was Susan Sinclair's first clue something was wrong. Kneeling in the dirt weeding her Cape Plumbago, she tightened her grip on the trowel in her hand, closed her eyes and prayed. "Please don't let this be happening again."

The sound of chewing, directly behind her, made her blood run cold. She took a deep breath and forced herself to turn around, her shaky hand clenching the trowel for dear life. Her eyes landed on a large silver belt buckle and a well-worn pair of blue jeans--not what she expected. She stood up slowly, her gaze traveling upwards until her brown eyes locked with the handsome stranger's blue eyes. He was grinning at her, his white teeth flashing as he chewed his gum.

He was taller than her, thin and lanky, with dark brown cowboy boots, a plaid shirt and a beige cowboy hat atop his collar-length brown, wavy hair. When he spoke, he drawled; his southern accent completing the image of a good-old southern boy.

"Hi, Susan, I'm Reed."

"Who are you and how do you know my name?" Susan's voice faltered and, irritated at her show of weakness, she thrust out her chin, daring him to test her. She shifted the trowel to her right hand, ready to defend herself if necessary. She was alone with a strange man, one who might be here to harm her. A stranger who knew her name.

"It's okay, Susan, he's with me." Susan's relief was palpable as she recognized U.S. Marshal Maggie Donahue's voice. A petite blonde woman wearing a white tank top, blue chambray shirt and faded blue jeans walked up from behind the man and shoved him playfully out of her way.

"This is my new partner, Reed." She walked over and wrapped her arms around the younger woman. "How are you?"

Susan returned the marshal's hug, but she held onto the trowel and kept her eye on the man, watching him over the woman's shoulder.

Reed shrugged. "I didn't mean to startle you," he

said, his voice deep and rich as molasses. "I was just checking out the yard and I found you here, tending your garden," he grinned and popped his gum.

The woman turned to her partner. "Don't make me regret vouching for you, Reed," she warned, her green eyes glittering in the sunshine.

He laughed and shook his head. "Maggie, you are a fine sister-in-law, but you sure can be a trial as a partner."

Susan was looking back and forth between the two of them, still feeling unsettled and not sure what was going on. "Sister-in-law?"

"Yeah, this pup is my husband's younger brother. And he's also my new partner. Jackson retired to be with his wife; they just found out she's got cancer," she added, a frown creasing her brow. "My sergeant said I could have my pick of the new U.S. Marshal recruits as a replacement partner, and this one here begged me to choose him," she grinned mischievously at Reed.

"It didn't hurt that I was top of my class in pretty much everything," he drawled. He turned to Susan and smiled, but when he looked over at Maggie, they both got serious. "I heard you've received some 'gifts' that got you spooked," he said. "We came over to check on you and see if you need to be relocated."

Susan sighed and nodded. "Why don't you come inside and have a lemonade? I'll show you what I've been getting." She set the trowel down at the edge of the flower bed, stood up and removed her gloves. She looked up at Reed, who was standing between her and the house.

Reed extended his arm for her to precede him, waiting until Maggie passed before falling in behind them. Susan led them into the house through the back door, motioning for them to have a seat at the small, round kitchen table while she walked over to the fridge.

As she reached inside, she wondered if she'd have to leave the home she'd worked so hard to make her own. She loved the red gingham curtains on the kitchen window, the plaid tablecloth, and the rooster and hen salt and pepper shakers sitting in the middle of the table. She sighed; she didn't want to move again, but she had to stay safe until the trial. She'd do anything to put Bruno DeLuca behind bars.

She set a pitcher, three glasses and a bowl of ice on a tray, then carried them over to the table. She snuck a look at Reed, who appeared to be admiring her salt and pepper shakers. He'd removed his cowboy hat and run his hand through his hair, so he didn't look nearly as intimidating as he had in the garden.

Susan gave him a tentative smile as she set the tray in front of him. "I know that Maggie doesn't like a lot of ice in her drink and I like to put *extra* ice in mine, so I figured I'd let you add as much or little as you'd like."

"Why thank you kindly," he replied, reaching for his glass. He scooped three ice cubes out of the bowl and poured himself some lemonade.

Susan looked over at Maggie. "Does he talk like that for real?" she asked.

Maggie sighed and shrugged her shoulders. "Unfortunately, yes."

"What's wrong with the way I talk?" Reed asked, making a face at Maggie. He sipped his drink. "Ahh, that hits the spot."

Maggie smiled tolerantly at her partner, then turned to Susan, her expression serious. "Why don't you show us what you got?"

Susan tasted her lemonade, trying to draw strength from the sweet-sour liquid, but she still felt anxious. She sighed and rose from the table. She grabbed a brown paper bag from the cupboard and dumped the contents onto the table.

Reed looked at the items, picked up one of the

bundles and sniffed at it. "These look and smell like rosemary." He looked up at Maggie with a puzzled expression on his face.

"I can see those wheels turning from here," she said to her partner. "Susan has a very good reason for finding these threatening."

Susan looked at him and nodded. "When I lived in New York, I had a roof-top garden where I grew herbs and vegetables. My mom loves to cook with rosemary, so I grew some to give her as a gift. I was picking rosemary and making bundles when I witnessed the murder. So, when these started appearing on my doorstep, it made me a little nervous."

He hung his head, reached over and grabbed her hand. "I got transferred to this case last night. Maggie briefed me this morning but I'm not aware of all the details, yet. I'm sorry you had to go through that, and I'm sorry if I scared you in the garden."

She pulled her hand back and tucked it in her lap, then looked him in the eye. "I was scared for a minute," she admitted, "but I figured if you chewed peppermint gum, you must be alright." They grinned at each other; a truce formed.

"All right, break it up, you two. We're not here for you to become besties, we're here to determine if you've been compromised." Maggie picked up one of the bundles. "How many of these have you received?"

"There have been four bundles," Susan replied. "I found the first one three days ago. It was on my front porch right outside the door when I got up. There's been one each day since, in the same spot. Then last night, there was one in the evening as well."

"Have you seen anyone strange hanging around lately?" Reed asked. When he saw the mischievous look in her eyes he quickly added, "besides me, I mean."

"No, I haven't," Susan replied with a grin. "I'm up early in the morning, and I check everything about ten times before I go to bed, so I know they're being left between 11 pm and 6 am. The second bundle was here when I got home from work, yesterday."

"Okay, that narrows it down quite a bit." Maggie's voice was thoughtful. "Do any of your neighbors have video doorbells or cameras or anything?"

"Not that I know of," she shrugged. "I didn't want to go around asking because it sounds strange and I didn't want anyone to know they'd rattled me."

"Have you received any unusual phone calls or emails?" Reed asked.

"No, the only thing out of the ordinary is the rosemary."

Maggie looked her in the eye. "Do you think you've been compromised?"

Susan looked from one concerned face to the other. "Not really," she shrugged. "But honestly, I'm not sure what to think."

The marshals exchanged a look. When his partner nodded, Reed spoke up. "We think it's too soon to tell. This could be a strange coincidence, or it could be something more sinister. We don't want to uproot you again if there's no need, but we also don't want you here by yourself, just in case."

Susan nodded and looked over at Maggie. "What are you suggesting, then?"

"We've decided that he's going to stay here with you, for the time being."

Susan's eyebrows raised and her mouth dropped open in horror. "But I'm a teacher at Sweet Grove Middle School," she exclaimed. "What will people think?"

They grinned as if they'd expected this reaction from her.

"Don't worry. I'll be posing as your brother," he

explained. "There's nothing wrong with your brother staying with you, is there?"

Susan was speechless. She'd never been alone with a man for more than a few minutes and her reputation was important to her. How would she cope with a strange man in her home? She looked over at Maggie and saw both concern and confidence on the marshal's face. They were just trying to keep her safe and she knew Maggie would never put her in a compromising situation.

She'd witnessed the brutal murder of a grown man and she didn't want to become another victim. If Maggie trusted Reed, she should be able to as well. Her decision made, she nodded at them. "Okay, I'll do it."

2

REED COULD FEEL the questions in the air as he and Susan walked into her classroom the next morning. Reed walked down the center aisle and sat at the back of the room while Susan--Miss Sinclair to her students--went to her desk at the front.

"Good morning everyone," she greeted her students.

"Good morning Miss Sinclair." Most of the students dutifully responded, but a few were too busy sneaking glances at the new guy.

Reed struggled with how to sit at the desk. His legs didn't quite fit underneath, so he had to sit with them sticking out into the aisle. He crossed his legs at the ankles and placed his hands on the desk, determined to be a good example.

"You might have noticed that we have a visitor today." Several heads turned to look at Reed who looked back with his best "aw shucks" look on his face. "This is my brother, Reed. He'll be staying with me for a while and he's going to be helping out in the classroom!" she announced. "Can we all wish him a good morning?"

The class responded with a raucous "Good morning!" followed by mangled versions of his name or "Miss Sinclair's brother." There was a wave of giggles from the girls while the boys either turned to stare at Reed or feigned indifference.

"Reed, would you like to say good morning to the class?" Susan asked, her eyes twinkling with mischief.

"Why certainly," he said. His deep voice caused a stir. The girls' eyes opened wide and the boys, whose voices hadn't changed yet, slunk down in their seats. "Good morning y'all! Thank you so much for the warm welcome!"

Hands quickly flew into the air, and Susan called on the student nearest herself. "Yes, Katy, you have a question?"

"Miss Sinclair why does your brother sound different than you?" Katy blushed when Reed turned his gaze her way and grinned at her.

"While my sister was studying and being a good child, I got into some trouble," he said, getting everyone's attention for the first time. "I got sent to live with my grandpappy, in the country, so I now I don't sound all uppity like my sister."

Susan bristled when Reed said she sounded uppity, but the students seemed to realize he was teasing her, and they all laughed at his antics. Even the boys seemed to be reacting to his charm, and the tension in the room eased slightly.

"All right then, on with today's lessons." Susan ignored the groans and started class.

REED SANK down into the sofa in the teacher's lounge with a groan of his own. He'd forgotten how uncomfortable school desks were. His 6'3" wiry frame wasn't meant for that kind of abuse. He was used to being on his feet all day, moving around. Sitting was not his forte.

"Oh my! You look lost," a throaty, female voice interrupted his thoughts. "I'd be more than happy to help you find your way."

"Back off, Brenda. That's my brother." Reed turned to look at Susan who was getting them each a cup of coffee. Her voice sounded tired and he wondered how she was holding up.

"Wonderful, then he's available!" Brenda sat down next to Reed on the sofa and he instinctively moved away. Unnaturally black hair piled high on her head, her blue eyes squinting as she looked at him, Brenda made Reed feel very uncomfortable. He decided right away that he'd rather face down a rattlesnake than deal with this snake in woman's body.

"Oh, stop, Brenda. For Pete's sake, act like a grown woman. Hi! I'm Jenny." A bright-eyed redhead sat down across from them. She gave Brenda a disapproving look and Reed a friendly smile.

"I'm Reed." He smiled back at her. "Nice to meet you."

"Nice to meet you, too! Susan never told me she had a brother."

"Well, I'm kinda the black sheep of the family," he drawled. He watched her eyes widen at the sound of his voice, and mentally sighed.

He'd been teased his whole life about the way he spoke, slowly drawing out his words. When he hit puberty, his deep voice became like a siren's call to women, making them swoon, and embarrassing him even more than the teasing had.

"Stop telling lies, Reed," Susan scolded. She handed him a cup of coffee then sat down next to Jenny. "Don't believe a word this one says, Jenny." She grinned at Jenny, then turned to Reed.

"This is my friend, so play nice."

"Yeah, play nice," Jenny repeated, nearly purring.

Reed smiled at Jenny, thinking she seemed nice. He looked over at Susan, but she was staring into her coffee, looking miserable, like the cheese had fallen off her cracker.

3

IT HAD BEEN a long day and Susan was tired. She was used to having time to herself and being with Reed all day had made her cranky. At least, that's what she told herself. She didn't want to examine the real reason she was feeling out of sorts. She glared out the window while Reed drove them back to her house.

"Your friends are nice, and your students really love you," Reed's voice broke the strained silence.

"They all seemed to love you, that's for sure." As soon as the words were out of her mouth, she sighed and turned to Reed. "I'm sorry. It's not your fault you made a big hit with all the women in Sweet Grove Middle School. I've never seen them so taken with anyone."

"Ah, Miss Sinclair. It's the drawl, is all," he laughed. "If it wasn't for this deep, sexy voice, no woman would even look at this ole' boy."

She knew he was teasing her, trying to lighten the mood; but she was still irritated. The day had been going so well, up until he'd met Jenny. She kept thinking about how her friend had looked at Reed, like he was a prime piece of beef. And he'd smiled back, lapping up the attention.

Susan had never been a jealous, envious person and she'd just met this man, so why was she feeling so possessive of him? And why had her heart ached when he'd smiled at Jenny?

Frustrated and angry with herself, she turned to look out the window, effectively ending the conversation. They rode the rest of the way in silence with Susan pretending to be captivated by the passing scenery. She didn't notice the glances Reed sent her way or the frown on his lips.

Reed pulled into her driveway and put his hand on her arm when she opened her car door. "Hang on for a minute, I want to check out the house first, make sure there are no surprises."

Susan swallowed hard and nodded. She'd almost forgotten why they were in this charade in the first place. He was a U.S. Marshal, there to protect her, nothing more. She needed to get a grip and stop acting like a silly school girl with a crush.

A whistle pierced the air and Susan looked out the windshield to see Reed motioning for her to join him on the porch. She grabbed her purse, got out of the car and slammed the door. She saw Reed's eyes widen at her display of temper, but she wasn't done yet.

"A whistle? Really? My daddy taught me that real men meet a lady at the door. They don't honk and they certainly don't whistle."

Susan watched an array of emotions pass across his face and knew she'd gone too far. She saw the sweet, nice guy retreat and a stranger take his place.

"My job is to keep you safe, ma'am," he said tersely, startling Susan with his formality. "There's a bundle of rosemary on your porch. I whistled because I need to keep you close while I check the house and I want you to keep an eye on the rosemary."

"That still doesn't explain why you whistled at me like I was your trained dog." She knew she was acting like a spoiled brat and she still wasn't sure why, but she couldn't help it. Reed's eyes narrowed and his frown grew deeper, but she met his eyes fearlessly.

He sighed and ran his hands through his hair, then in a calm, yet formal voice said, "I'm a trained U.S. Marshal. I'm not here to take you to dinner, I'm here to keep you safe. What I do might not make sense to you, but I have my reasons. I need you to trust me and follow my instructions."

Her eyes filled with tears. "I'm sorry, Reed. I know all that. It's just. . .everything!" she cried out. She took a couple of deep, ragged breaths while Reed stood nearby, watching her, hands in his pockets.

Get it together, Susan! she told herself. This was not who she was. She could examine her out-of-character behavior later, but right now it she needed to act like a grown-up. She took another breath, wiping her eyes with the back of her hand. She squared her shoulders and looked up at him, her eyes red, but full of determination. "What do you want me to do?" she asked.

"That's the spirit," he encouraged her, sounding more like the friendly man she'd spent the day with. "I need you to stand right here so you can see into the house and still keep an eye on the street. If anything seems wrong or unusual, I want you to call out and I'll come running. I need to check out the inside of the house and make sure there are no other surprises."

He leaned forward, lifted her chin with his fingers and looked her in the eye. "Don't worry Miss Sinclair, I'll be back quicker than a hot knife through butter," he drawled, making her giggle in spite of herself.

Reed searched the house and while she kept an eye on the rosemary, she reflected on her behavior. She'd seen other women act crazy over a man and she'd never understood it. Now it was happening to her and she *really* didn't understand it. Regardless of her reaction to him, she had to remember he was here to keep her safe, not date her.

It wasn't long before he rejoined her on the porch. "All clear inside. It's safe to go in."

"Praise the Lord," she said softly, "I need a hot bath and a nice, home-cooked meal."

"Well, you go on and take that bath. I checked out your fridge last night and I found the makin's for some good grub. That is, if you don't mind cooking for you?" he asked.

She eyed him suspiciously. "You seem too good to be true. You protect and serve and cook, too? And by the way, your drawl and accent seem to come and go an awful lot," she said. "Is any of that persona real?"

Reed grinned and winked at her. "It's all real,

honey, but sometimes, I add a little extra to spice things up!"

Susan didn't want him calling her 'honey,' at least not like this, but she knew he was trying to diffuse the tension, and he was so cute and charming she couldn't be angry with him.

"Fine, you can cook dinner. But don't call me honey."

"Yes ma'am, Miss Sinclair," he saluted her, his eyes sparkling.

She headed for her bedroom, shaking her head and wondering why the way he said Miss Sinclair made her heart race.

4

IT WAS AMAZING how a nice hot bubble bath could turn a bad day around. Susan finished drying her hair and added one last swipe of mascara. She looked in the mirror and almost didn't recognize herself.

She'd always worn her blonde hair short, but now, in WITSEC, she had a new name and a new look. Besides the auburn-colored hair and longer, wavier hairstyle, there were worry lines and dark circles that hadn't been there a few months ago. But she also saw a more mature, stronger woman.

She sighed and turned towards the door. Just as she reached for the knob, there was a knock. She opened the door and was surprised to find Reed standing there, a tray of food in his hands.

"I thought you might prefer to have your dinner in here, so you don't have to put up with me anymore today." His twinkling eyes let her know he was teasing, but she realized there was an ugly element of truth to it.

"I'm not putting up with you," she corrected. "I'm just not used to being around people all day, every day. I like to have some time alone, away from people."

"Believe me, I understand the need for some privacy. I grew up with four brothers and three sisters. When I could afford to move out, I got my own little studio apartment. My brothers wanted me to share a place with them and they couldn't understand why I refused. But I needed some peace and quiet, a place where I could just relax and be alone." He suddenly stopped talking and looked down at her, his eyes wide. He probably hadn't meant to share so much personal information and she struggled to find a way to let him know she respected his honesty.

"Now that I've had a nice bath, I'd actually appreciate some company, if you don't mind," she broke the awkward silence.

He nodded, "Happy to oblige, Miss Sinclair."

She followed him to the dining table and sat down. "Would you like to say grace or should I?" she asked.

"It's your home, so it's your choice." His nonchalant response riled her up again and just as she was about to let him have it for being rude, he ducked his head, closed his eyes and started the prayer.

"Dear Lord, thank You for the food, for the company and for another day on this earth. We appreciate You providing for us and keeping us safe. In Your name, amen."

He took the platter from the tray and set it in front of Susan. Her mouth started to water at the tantalizing aroma of the chicken fried steak, mashed potatoes, green beans and gravy.

"You made this?" she asked, incredulous. "From what I had in my kitchen?"

Reed laughed. "Yes, I did. You didn't have the spices I normally use, but I improvised. I think it turned out pretty darn good!"

Susan picked up a fork and knife and sliced off a piece of the chicken fried steak. As she took a bite, she moaned in pleasure. "Oh my! This is wonderful!"

His face flushed, and even the tops of his ears

turned pink with embarrassment. "Do you really like it?"

Susan could tell that it meant a lot to him, and it really was delicious, so she smiled and nodded. "I really do! This is amazing." She took a bite of the mashed potatoes and the green beans. "Wow! These are incredible, too!"

He sat down and started eating his supper. "Oh yeah, I like this. I hope I can remember how I made this. It's even better than usual." He took another bite, then looked up at Susan who was watching him. He swallowed his food, wiped his mouth on his napkin, then asked, "What? Why are you looking at me like that?"

"Better than usual?" she repeated. "You make this regularly?"

"Well, yeah, don't you?" His brow creased in confusion as he looked at her.

"No!" she laughed. "I live alone. I usually eat soup or a sandwich or make a cheese plate."

He looked at her, aghast. "A cheese plate? Now it's my turn to say, 'really?'" he joked. She grinned at him and took another bite of her food. "Seriously, though. You don't cook meals for yourself?"

She pushed some potatoes around on her plate

while she thought. "I used to," she admitted. "But I'm tired when I get home and I hate wasting food. I'm not much of a leftover person, so if I make more than I can eat at one sitting, it usually goes to waste."

"Well, I'll just have to teach you how to make this wonderful dinner for one, then. That way you can make it often and not have an excuse to make a cheese plate!" He shuddered in mock horror.

She shook her head and laughed. "If you can teach me to cook food that tastes like this, I give you my word I'll give up cheese plates forever!" she vowed.

"Challenge accepted," he rubbed his hands together gleefully.

REED WAS EXHAUSTED. He wanted to go straight to bed but he needed to patrol before he settled in for the night. He let himself out the front door and locked it behind him. He looked up and down the neighborhood street. Most of the houses were dark at this hour, but a couple still had lights burning in at least one room. It was quiet tonight, the sound of crickets notwithstanding.

He turned and looked at Susan's home. It was a nice house. The outside was painted medium blue with white shutters and a white fence encircled the small front yard. The garden ran along the front of the house, then down the side and into the back, with flowers of all colors and green ornamental grasses which gave it an organic, unplanned look. Both the front and back yards sported a well-trimmed lawn of buffalo grass, creating an interesting contrast of order next to the wild garden.

He'd never had a home like this, and he'd always been a bit envious of those who did. Family was important to him, and he hoped that one day he'd have a house filled with children and wife who loved him. He wanted a yard and trees and friendly neighbors he could invite over for a weekend barbecue. It was nice dream, but he wasn't sure if a life like that was in the cards for this U.S. Marshal.

Reed sighed. He'd finished checking the outside of the house and now it was time to get to bed. He would be going to school with Susan in the morning and if today was any indication, he'd need his rest. He'd forgotten how noisy classrooms were and how rambunctious kids were. It was more than that, though. Even though women were attracted to him wherever he went, dealing with the women in the teacher's lounge had stressed him out. It'd never bothered him until today. Somehow, knowing Susan was watching made the attention embarrassing instead of flattering.

He walked up the steps and unlocked the front door. He shut it behind him and made sure the deadbolt was secure. As he walked past her closed bedroom door, he thought about how scared she must have been, witnessing a brutal murder and being forced to leave her life behind. She'd just started to get settled in when the bundles of rosemary appeared on her doorstep. He must have scared the daylights out of her when he walked up behind her while she was gardening. Dealing with all of that would be hard for anyone, so he would try harder to understand her mood swings.

That still didn't explain why she'd been surly on the ride home and why she'd snapped at him when he whistled. To be fair, he'd tried to get her attention, but she was staring in the other direction. At the time, a whistle had seemed more discreet that yelling, "Hey Susan, come watch the stuff the perp left!"

Reed chuckled to himself as he put on his pajamas. He'd try to remember what she was going through and cut her some slack. He was a nice guy, but his job wasn't to make her smile, or protect her feelings. It was to keep her safe.

Even so, his last thought before he fell asleep was of how Susan's eyes sparkled when she smiled at him, and how she made his heart race.

5

SUSAN WOKE up to the smell of coffee brewing and some sort of sugary scent that she couldn't quite identify. She rolled over and looked at her alarm clock. It wasn't due to go off for another 20 minutes.

She sat up and stretched, marveling at the fact that she wasn't angry. Normally, if she woke up before her alarm, she'd be irritated. But the aromas coming from her kitchen were winning her over and she hurried to get dressed.

She walked out of her bedroom 15 minutes later. She could smell bacon now, and her mouth watered in anticipation. Reed's back was to her as she walked into the kitchen and as she watched him turn the bacon in the skillet, she took a moment to reflect.

She'd lived alone most of her life. She preferred

to take care of herself and was usually uncomfortable around others. Her mother had teased her about becoming a teacher and being surrounded by people all day, since she was such an introvert. But kids were different, she'd argued. She didn't feel overwhelmed in front of her class, she felt invigorated. Being around adults, that's what made her sweat.

He turned around and smiled at her, catching her off-guard. She blushed and smiled back, tentatively. "I can smell bacon and coffee, but I can't identify the other amazing smell," she said as she walked towards him.

"Blueberry muffins." He gestured towards the table with the tongs. "Have a seat and I'll get you a plate." Susan started to argue--it was her kitchen after all, and he shouldn't be ordering her around. But her stomach chose that moment to rumble loudly, so she retreated to the table, hoping he hadn't heard.

There were coffee mugs on the table along with a steaming carafe of coffee, so she poured herself a cup. He'd placed some cream and sugar on the table as well and she helped herself to a spoonful of sugar and a splash of cream. She slowly took a sip of the hot liquid.

"Oh, my goodness, this is the best coffee I've ever

tasted!" She took another sip and was delighted to find it tasted just as amazing as her first sip.

She looked up when a plate was placed in front of her with a large muffin and four perfectly cooked slices of bacon. "Thank you, Reed." She marveled at the beauty of the blueberry muffin. She wanted to take a bite, but she needed to do something first.

He joined her at the table, reaching across and laying his hand next to hers, leaving it up to her if she took it or not. She wrapped her fingers around his large hand and held tight.

"Thank You, Lord, for the food and the heavenly coffee. Thank You for bringing me a marshal who can cook and who knows how to clean up after himself. Bless us and keep us safe this fine day, amen."

Susan picked up the muffin and took a large bite. Her eyes opened wide in amazement as the incredible flavors of blueberry and butter hit her taste buds and he grinned at her reaction.

He grabbed one for himself and just as he bit into the muffin, there was a loud knock at the door. Reed finished chewing, took off the apron he'd been wearing and set it on the counter.

"That'll be Maggie," he said as he walked

towards the door. "She wanted to check in with you and make sure you're still okay with me being here."

She choked on the muffin and grabbed a napkin to cover her mouth. Had her childish behavior yesterday made him reconsider staying with her? She stood up and rushed to the door, stopping dead in her tracks as she reached it.

Reed was standing on the porch looking down at Maggie who was squatting and bagging another bundle of rosemary. "I was out here an hour ago and that wasn't there," she heard him say.

"I believe you. Everything has dew on it but the rosemary, which means it hasn't been here long." She sighed, looking up into Susan's stricken eyes. "Did either of you hear anything at all?"

Reed looked over at Susan and she shook her head, no. He shrugged his shoulders and stuck his hands in his pockets. "I'm going to walk around the yard and the street, see if I see anything out of place."

The women watched him walk away and Maggie shook her head. "I was really hoping Reed's presence would deter this person, but I guess not."

"He's only been here for a day," she reminded her. "Maybe they didn't notice him yet." She shrugged her shoulders and was so focused on watching him walk away she missed the grin on Maggie's face and the glint in her eye.

"So, you're okay with Reed staying? Even though you got another bundle of rosemary?"

"Of course. It's not his fault. Let's give it more time and see what happens," she suggested. She heard the marshal cough, looked over at her and did a double take. "What? Why are you grinning at me like that?"

"Oh, nothing," Maggie told her. "I'm just surprised that you're okay with him staying, that's all." Susan felt her cheeks start to flush and turn pink, and she ducked her head in embarrassment.

"I've never lived with a man," she admitted. "I thought it would be uncomfortable and awkward. But Reed cooked dinner last night and made me breakfast this morning, which was amazing. I slept better than I've slept in a long time, knowing he was here, keeping watch over me." She paused, shrugging her shoulders. "I don't know. Maybe I've just been alone too long."

"Maybe," Maggie said, her voice thoughtful. "Or maybe it's his charm winning you over." She grinned cheekily at Susan who blushed furiously.

"What's going on here?" Reed asked. He climbed the porch steps looking from his partner's laughing face to Susan's beet-red face. She didn't have an answer for that, so she fled into the house, mumbling something about being late for school.

Safely behind the closed door of her bedroom, she looked at herself in the mirror. She knew she'd been rude, but she'd been startled by the realization that Maggie might be right. What if she was falling for Reed? That couldn't end well. For one thing, he was posing as her brother. For another, if they didn't find out who was leaving her little presents, she'd have to start over again, somewhere else, as someone else and she'd never see him again.

She made a face at herself in the mirror. "Get a grip, Susan. He's not your boyfriend, he's the muscle." She laughed as she pictured him flexing his biceps in his cowboy hat and boots, and she relaxed a little.

Susan noticed her bedside clock in the mirror's reflection and realized she'd better get a move on or she really was going to be late for school. She finished getting ready in record time and headed into the kitchen. She wasn't about to leave without finishing her delicious breakfast.

6

HOW DID I MISS IT? Reed wondered for the umpteenth time. He'd been so focused on making a nice breakfast he hadn't been paying attention. That was a rookie mistake and one he couldn't let happen again. This woman deserved his protection and he had to keep his marshal hat on at all times.

It was hard though, he admitted to himself. She was sweet and cute and funny. And she was so skittish. But when he cooked for her, she relaxed, and he thoroughly enjoyed watching her eat. He'd never seen anyone so prim and proper eat like Susan did-- enjoying every bite.

Aw dang, I did it again! The two seconds he'd spent thinking about Susan were two seconds where he'd let his guard down. If that happened again, he'd have to tell Maggie he couldn't protect Susan. That admission could cost him his job. "I'd rather lose my job than let anything happen to my witness," he whispered.

"Are you ready to go to school?" Susan's voice broke into his reverie, startling him. He turned and looked into her eyes, but he couldn't tell if she'd heard him talking to himself. He decided the safest course of action was to act like nothing had happened, so he nodded and replied, "I'm ready as I'll ever be."

She stopped and looked at him intently, a frown on her face. She set her purse and jacket on the table and walked up to him, her eyes searching his.

"You didn't do anything wrong, Reed," she said, her voice kind, yet firm. "Neither of us heard a thing. If you're at fault, then so am I," she raised her chin and dared him to contradict her.

Again, she'd impressed him. She wasn't caving in to her fears, so he couldn't let her see his doubts. "Okay, then, I won't beat myself up about it," he told her, crossing his fingers behind his back. He'd say anything to make her feel safe and keep her from looking at him with disappointment.

"Mm hmm," she replied. She turned and grabbed her things then walked towards the front door. She paused as her hand touched the doorknob. "Did you and Maggie remove the rosemary or is it still there?"

"Maggie took it with her. She decided to see if she could lift any prints or DNA off the leaves or the ribbon they're tied with." Her pinched look relaxed and she nodded as she opened the door.

She really is a brave woman, he thought. Most of the time she didn't even seem scared, but it was the little things that gave her away. He was grateful she trusted him enough to show her fear.

"OKAY, class, that's it for today," Susan announced. Her words were met with cheers and the rustle of students putting their books away.

"Are we still meeting today?" a quiet voice caught her attention. She turned to look into the cool, green eyes of her student, Mary. "I mean, if you're too busy . . ." her voice trailed off as she frowned and dropped her eyes.

She reached out and placed her hand on the young woman's shoulder. "Of course, we're meeting, Mary. I'm never too busy for you."

Reed was in the back of the room and he looked

up, meeting her eyes. He walked towards them; his long legs stiff from sitting at the desk. "I need to move around a bit and loosen up. I'll meet you in the break room when you're done, sis."

He smiled at Mary who ducked her head and looked away. He met Susan's eyes and looked at her pointedly, reminding her he'd be keeping an eye on her. She nodded and walked him to the door. She closed the door after him and turned to face her student.

"So, what are we doing today? Did you bring the application forms?" Mary liked to take pictures, and she'd been encouraging the girl to enter her photos in contests. She figured it would help build her confidence and she was so talented; Susan knew she could win.

The girl hesitated. "I know you're busy, Miss Sinclair. You don't have to help me. I can figure this out myself."

"Of course, you can," Susan shrugged. "But you don't have to. I've been looking forward to seeing which photos you've chosen to submit." She sat down next to Mary and scooted her chair closer so she could see better.

Mary still looked unsure, so she reached over and opened her portfolio. "Oh wow! This one is amazing;

you've captured the exact moment the sun set behind the library."

She smiled at her teacher and the sparkle returned to her eyes. They settled in and discussed the pros and cons of each of her photos.

REED WAS ENGROSSED in the article on his laptop when he heard someone clear her throat. He looked up and saw it was Susan's friend, Jenny. He closed the laptop and grinned up at the woman.

"Well now, I can't believe your sister just left you here, all alone," she simpered. She fluffed her red hair then placed her hand on her hip, causing her red silk blouse to strain across her chest.

He plastered on a fake smile but wished he didn't have to waste time talking with the woman. This assignment had been thrown at him last minute and he was reviewing all of the case files and newspaper articles to catch up and see if they'd missed anything. If it had been Brenda, he would have told her he was too busy to talk, but this woman was Susan's friend, so he figured he should be polite.

"I'm not alone, I've got you here to keep me

company." Reed mentally groaned when her cheeks turned pink and her eyes lit up at his words.

He gestured for her to have a seat across the table from him but wasn't all that surprised when she sat in the chair next to him, then scooted it closer. He was glad he'd had the foresight to close the laptop. It could have been a disaster if Jenny had seen the article and learned Susan's true identity.

He'd been reading a news article about the attack Susan had witnessed. It detailed the murder and gave an accounting of the murderer's criminal history. It was clear this guy was dangerous and not the kind to leave any loose strings. Once again, he was amazed by how well she was dealing with everything, all on her own.

He pushed his chair back and rested one foot on his knee, effectively creating a physical barrier between himself and Jenny. He watched her face as she assessed the situation, the left side of her mouth dipping down in irritation. Reed wanted to laugh, but he didn't want to hurt her feelings, so he sat quietly, waiting for her to speak.

"So, where is your lovely sister this fine afternoon?" she asked. Her voice dripped with contrived interest as she tried to maneuver closer to Reed.

"She had a meeting with one of her students."

He crossed his arms over his chest and leaned back in the chair.

"Oh, yes, little Miss Mary." Reed's interest was piqued. Jenny's tone was venomous, and she seemed like she wanted to share, so he decided to encourage her. He might learn something helpful in the process.

"You don't like Mary?" he asked.

"She's a drama queen," Jenny said, rolling her eyes. Her face turned pink as soon as the words were out of her mouth, and she quickly added, "I mean, she lost her mom recently and she's been having a rough go of it. Susan spends time with her and encourages her photography, but I mean, we all know it's a waste of time."

"Really? Why would that be a waste of time?" Reed felt himself getting annoyed, but he wanted to know why she was so willing to write off a child's future. He smiled slowly at her and raised an eyebrow, his charm effectively flustering the woman. He could see the pulse in her throat speed up as he leaned closer. "Just between the two of us," he whispered, his voice even deeper and raspier than usual.

"Oh my," she said, "did it just get hotter in here or what?" She fanned herself furiously for a moment while Reed waited patiently. "Well, the thing is, her daddy killed her ma. Right in front of her. And then she turned on him and told the cops." Jenny took a breath and leaned towards Reed, lowering her voice as she shared her conclusion. "Coming from a trashy family like that, well, she isn't going to be going very far, if you know what I mean."

Reed sat back in his chair slowly, trying very hard to keep his emotions from showing on his face. *How dare she!* he thought. *How dare she talk about the poor girl that way.* Reed despised people who gossiped and acted superior. God didn't see people that way and Reed believed that God judged people by the way they treated others, not by who they were unfortunate enough to be related to.

But the woman wasn't done. "I told Susan it was stupid to help that girl, but Susan just kept at it and ignored me." She sniffed and paused for a moment, waiting for Reed to agree with her. When he didn't say anything, she narrowed her eyes. "Don't tell me you agree with your sister?"

"I absolutely agree with my sister," Reed replied. He stood up slowly and tried to keep from clenching his fists as he looked down into her face. "Everyone is worth helping. It doesn't matter who their parents were or what they did. What matters is what they do today and how they treat people. I think you might want to take a hard look at yourself before you go around judging others."

Reed placed his hat on his head, picked up his laptop and walked away as she gaped, her mouth flopping open and shut. As he walked towards Susan's classroom, he couldn't keep the grin off his face. People like that made him angry and he was glad he'd been able to tell her what he thought, although he was certain there would be repercussions.

7

"THESE ARE REALLY GOOD, MARY." Susan clapped her hands excitedly. "Your photos capture the subjects perfectly and I think you've chosen the best ones to submit. I can't wait to help you with the essay part on Friday, when we meet again."

This particular contest required seven photos along with an essay explaining why the photographer chose those photos and what they mean to him or her. Mary had expressed her uncertainty about writing the essay and Susan had offered to help her.

Mary grinned at her teacher and started to say something, but there was a sharp rap at the door and Reed stuck his head in.

"Sorry to interrupt, I just wanted to let you know I'll be waiting out here in the hallway."

Mary's smile turned to a frown. She ducked her head and grabbed the pictures, stuffing them into her backpack. Susan frowned. *What is that about?* she wondered.

"No worries, Reed, we're just finishing up here," she told him, still watching her student's face. Reed looked at her with a question in his eyes, but she just shook her head at him. He nodded and headed for the back of room, where he usually sat.

"I'm proud of you, Mary," she said softly.

She looked at her and nodded. "Thanks Miss Sinclair. I'll see you in the morning." She picked up her backpack and walked out of the room.

"Was it something I said?" Reed asked, breaking her out of her trance.

"I honestly don't know," she replied. "We were doing fine then all of a sudden, she got quiet and withdrew. She's been going through a lot, but I thought she was getting better."

"Jenny just told me some of it. That poor girl," he said, shaking his head. "It's amazing she's functioning at all."

She shrugged her shoulders. "Human beings can be amazing, but they can also be horrible."

"Speaking of horrible, I might have created a situation in the break room." His voice sounded regretful, but she saw a flash of anger in his eyes and realized that whatever it was, he was still fuming.

"Why don't you tell me about it over dinner," she suggested. "I'm famished!"

"That sounds like a plan." He grinned and she could see some of his tension ease. "What sounds good?"

They discussed their options as they walked to the car and had narrowed it down to Mexican or burgers when Reed suddenly stopped and thrust his arm in front of her. He turned and moved in close to her, his hand reaching into his jacket.

"Stay here and don't move," he hissed. His eyes were scanning the parking lot as he pulled his gun out of its holster, holding it down near his thigh. He looked into her eyes and whispered, "I mean it."

Susan gulped and nodded, then held her breath as he approached her car. He scanned the area around the car, then looked underneath it. He stood up and looked at something on the hood. He pulled a pen from his pocket and poked at something. He looked around again, then motioned for her to join him. She saw him discretely tuck the gun into the waistband of his pants.

Her heart raced and her hands and knees were shaking. She wasn't sure she wanted to see what he'd found, but she forced herself to move towards him, keeping her eyes on his strong, handsome face for courage. As she passed the driver's door, she saw something resting on the hood. Reed was alternately watching her and looking around, and when she reached him, he put his hand on her arm.

"I don't know if we're being watched or not, so try not to react. Just look down, then get in the car like it's nothing," he advised. His voice was low, but she could tell he was angry.

She looked down and saw a piece of paper. She shifted to see it better. It was drawing of a man that looked an awful lot like Reed. The eyes had been scratched out and under the drawing were the words, "He needs to go, now!"

Chills ran down Susan's spine and she felt sick to her stomach. She felt his hand squeeze her arm and remembered his instructions. She looked up into his eyes and nodded, letting him know she was okay. She got into the driver's seat and started the car while Reed picked up the paper by the corner, walked around and climbed in the passenger side.

She pulled out of the parking lot and continued towards the center of town. "What do I do now," she asked. She was acting brave, but her voice quivered, revealing her fear.

"Just keep driving around. I'll let you know when I've determined we're clear." He tucked the offensive drawing into his backpack, trying to touch only the edges so he didn't get his fingerprints all over it.

Susan drove through town, taking some side streets she was familiar with, so she didn't get herself lost. She drove past one of the restaurants they'd discussed and realized she wasn't up to eating out. "Can we just go home for dinner?" she asked. "I don't think I can handle being in public right now."

"Of course, we can," he answered. "I'm sure I can find something to whip up. How do you feel about a western omelet? I think you have everything I need."

Her head whipped around, and she stared at him. "How can you be so calm and act like everything's normal?" she asked, her voice rising as she started to panic. But his strong hand on her arm calmed her down once again.

She took a deep breath and looked over at Reed. "Okay, I get it. Act normal, don't fall apart. Until we're behind closed doors; because once we're behind closed doors, all bets are off," she declared.

She heard Reed's chuckle and gave him a dirty look, but he was looking in the rearview mirror and didn't see. "Okay. I haven't seen anyone following us. I think it's safe to head to your house now."

REED HAD her wait in the car until he signaled her to join him on the porch. "So far, so good," he told her as she walked up the steps. "Now stay here and I'll check the inside."

"I know, I know," Susan muttered.

He looked down at her and had the strongest urge to pull her into his arms. He wasn't sure if he wanted to comfort her or himself. He would never admit it, but the image of himself with the eyes scratched out had shaken him to the core. He was supposed to be protecting her, not making things worse.

He walked through each room, hand on his gun, until he was certain they were clear. He walked to the front door and gestured for Susan to come in.

She sighed and headed immediately for the fridge. "I don't know about you, but I could definitely use a tall, icy glass of lemonade right now."

"That sounds good. If you don't mind, though, I'm going to walk around the yard really quick," he said. "I'll be back in a few."

"Say hi to Maggie for me," Susan said sweetly, turning to smirk at Reed.

"Busted." Reed looked her in the eye, assessing her emotional state. "I need to let her know what happened, but I don't want to upset you."

Susan shrugged. She turned and poured two glasses of lemonade, adding ice and straws. She set them on the table and sat down, sliding one glass towards him. She looked up at Reed, a determined expression on her face. "I appreciate your consideration, but I'd rather hear what you two have to say than be left in the dark. I'd like to have some input on our next move."

His admiration for her grew even more. He watched her face as she lifted her drink and placed the straw between her lips. Annoyed with himself for thinking about his witness's lips, he cleared his throat, sat down at the table and called his partner.

"Hey Maggie, you're on speaker." Susan looked at him with her eyebrow raised, but he just shrugged. "It's a cop thing," he said. She continued to look at him and he felt his cheeks redden under her scrutiny.

"He's right, Susan," Maggie's voice came from the phone speaker. "That's what we're taught to do any time we're not alone. Don't take it personal."

"Mm hm." her noncommittal reply made him grin.

"Anyhoo, I'm calling because we had another incident and Susan wants to be part of our next step." He explained about the picture they'd found and how he'd handled it. He took a sip of his lemonade and waited for her to respond, knowing she was considering all the angles.

"That's an escalation." She sounded concerned, but also excited. "I think that means we're on to something. We must have spooked somebody."

"I thought that, too, at first," Susan piped in. "But who? This seems out of character for men who kill without remorse. This seems more personal, more emotional."

He grinned at her and they could hear Maggie chuckle. "I told you she was special, Reed." She looked up at him, her eyes wide and her cheeks pink.

'Yes, ma'am, she is definitely special," he drawled. For a moment, their eyes met and held.

"Alrighty then," Maggie's matter-of-fact voice broke the tension. "We need a new plan. One that makes it clear Reed's not going anywhere."

"Are you sure?" His voice was hesitant, and Susan frowned. "I mean, if I'm riling this person up, could I be increasing the risk to Susan?"

Maggie sighed. "So far the only threat has been to you. The rosemary hasn't been sent with any type of warning or threat. I'm inclined to think that whoever this is isn't interested in hurting her. At least, not at the moment."

All three were silent, considering the options.

"I think I'd like to keep things the way they are for right now," Susan said. "Obviously Reed being here has changed something, but until we know what, I feel better having him close."

He felt like his heart was going to burst out of his chest. His mind told him she felt safer because he was a U.S. Marshal, but his heart rejoiced at the thought that she valued him, as a person, maybe even as a man.

Trying hard not to grin, he spoke up. "I'm with her. I'd like to keep going and see what happens."

His partner was silent for a moment as she thought it through. "Okay, then, we're agreed. We'll leave things the same for now. But both of you need to be extra alert and vigilant. We don't know who we're dealing with yet, so don't do anything stupid."

"Thanks partner. I'll talk to you later. I need to whip up some dinner. Susan's famished." He grinned at Susan and she nodded her head in agreement.

Maggie laughed. "Have him make you an omelet, Susan. I don't know how he does it, but they come out fluffy and delicious. Take care you two. Talk to you later."

He hung up the phone and turned to Susan. "What would you like for dinner?"

"You heard Maggie," she laughed. "After that endorsement, how can I say no?"

"Okay, then. Omelets it is!"

SUSAN CHANGED out of her school clothes and into jeans and a T-shirt. She'd always been independent and self-sufficient, so it surprised her that she enjoyed having Reed cook for her. She also felt a little guilty. He was on duty 24/7 taking care of her. The least she could do was help him in the kitchen.

She caught sight of herself in the mirror as she walked across the room. Her cheeks were rosy, and her eyes were bright. Her lips were curved in a smile and she admitted to herself that having him around wasn't the hardship she'd expected it to be. She fluffed her hair, then messed it up again. *This isn't a date*, she reminded herself. But the woman in her didn't care. She fluffed her hair again and added a touch of lip gloss. Satisfied, she headed for the kitchen.

"Hey, that smells delicious!" she exclaimed as she joined him at the stove.

"What can I say," he teased, "I'm impressive."

She couldn't think of an appropriate response, so she lifted the lid on the skillet and took a peek. Home fries with small chunks of onion, red and green bell pepper tantalized her senses, making her mouth water. She reached for a fork, planning to sample the dish.

"Don't you dare!" he playfully slapped at her wrist as she reached for the utensil. She pouted, but he just laughed. "Have a seat at the table and I'll bring the food over. Or better yet, if you could set the table while I finish cooking, I'd really appreciate it."

She set the table and sat down, her taste buds on high alert. She nearly started drooling when Reed set plates of home fries, omelets, bacon and sausage in the middle of the table.

REED KNEW he would never get tired of her excitement at his cooking. He liked food and he liked eating, but he didn't appreciate it like she did. He was used to cooking for himself or for Maggie and his brother, who enjoyed his food but didn't swoon over it. He had to admit he enjoyed having someone who relished everything he made.

He watched her eyes widen and her lips part as he set the serving dishes on the table. There he went again, thinking of her lips. He had to stop doing that. Now she was looking at him with a 'hurry up' expression. What did she want from him?

"Sit down and take my hand," she demanded. Confused, Reed stood still, staring at her. "I want to eat, and we need to say grace." She held out her hand and looked up at him, her eyes pleading with him to quit dawdling.

"Right," Reed replied. He sat and took her hand in his, glad she didn't hesitate to touch him anymore. They bowed their heads and Susan said grace quickly, letting go of his hand too soon.

"You get started," he told her. "I'll be right back."

As Reed stood up, Susan's worried face caught his eye. "I just want to walk around the house really quick. I'll lock the door behind me, so you have nothing to be concerned about." Susan bit her lip and nodded, making his heart sink. She'd been so happy a minute ago and now he'd ruined her mood.

He sighed and leaned down to look Susan in the

eye. "It don't amount to a hill o' beans. I just don't want my sister-in-law to get her britches in a tangle." He spoke in his best, southern drawl, hoping to make her laugh.

Susan's gaze held his, and he could see the wheels turning. Apparently satisfied that he was telling the truth, she nodded. "Fine, but if all the bacon gets eaten before you get back, it's your fault." She grinned impishly at him as she grabbed a piece of bacon and took a bite.

"If you eat all that bacon before I get back, I'm pretty sure you're going to end up with a tummy ache." He laughed when she responded by shrugging her shoulders and taking another bite. "Fine, I'll hurry," he conceded.

She shrugged and reached for the home fries, scooping a big pile on her plate. He headed out as she grabbed the omelets, afraid she might not be joking and there wouldn't be any food left if he took too long.

He checked the outside of the house and walked the perimeter. The street was quiet, neighbors all settled in for the evening. Feeling more confident about their safety, he went back inside to eat his dinner—if there was any left.

8

"SETTLE DOWN CLASS!" Susan called out over the din. "It's time to get back to work." A collective groan met her ears, led by none other than Reed, from the back of the room.

"This is my classroom and if you can't behave, I'll send you to the principal's office," she said sternly, looking directly at her "brother."

"Ooh, snap!" one of the students whispered, as others giggled and turned to stare at an unrepentant Reed.

"Is that supposed to scare me?" he whispered to the student nearest him, who gulped and immediately looked to Miss Sinclair for help.

"Reed, enough," she said. "The rest of you, open your books to Chapter 10, page 126." She picked up her marker and wrote the assignment on the white board at the front of the class. She turned back to the class and realized that two of the young men were alternately staring at Reed then whispering to each other. She looked at Reed and he nodded, letting her know he was aware. Since he was paying attention, Susan tried to relax and get back into teacher mode.

"Katy, would you please read the first paragraph on page 126? And when Katy is done, we'll go down the row with each of you reading one paragraph. Okay?" Her question was met with grumbles by everyone but Katy and Mary, who loved reading aloud. Katy sat up, cleared her throat and waited until her teacher nodded to begin reading.

Susan tried to pay attention, but it was difficult. She found herself sneaking peeks at the boys in the back of the classroom and looking over at Reed. When the second student finished reading and the room went quiet, waiting for a response from their distracted teacher, Susan had to admit defeat.

"I'm sorry class, I'm feeling a little off today. How about we put our books aside and have free time for the last 15 minutes of class." Her words were met with whoops of joy and the classroom quickly devolved into a free-for-all.

Susan looked up to see Katy walking towards

her. "Are you okay, Miss Sinclair?" The girl's brow was furrowed, and she seemed anxious, twisting her hands in front of her.

"I'm fine, Katy, thanks for asking." The girl didn't look convinced, so she added, "I didn't sleep well last night, and I think it's catching up with me, that's all."

The girl nodded and leaned forward. "I hate when I don't sleep well. It leaves me feeling like my head's all full of fog."

"That's it, exactly," she agreed. "I'm sure I'll sleep tonight and be back to normal tomorrow."

Susan sighed. It was true. She hadn't slept well. For the first time in a long time, she'd dreamt about Bruno DeLuca, the man she was set to testify against. He'd gone after Reed and Maggie and she'd been unable to do anything to help them. She'd woken up drenched in sweat, her heart racing. The dream had left her feeling anxious and unsettled; if anything happened to them because of her, she'd never forgive herself.

She rubbed her tired eyes and looked over at Reed. He was surrounded by students who were watching him make animals and flowers out of paper. He explained that he was doing origami and he patiently answered every question the students asked.

He really is an amazing man, she thought. Handsome, smart, funny and talented; too bad she hadn't met him before her life turned upside down. As if he felt her watching him, Reed looked up and smiled at her, making her heart flutter and her breath catch in her throat.

Susan quickly looked away, hoping it wasn't obvious how he affected her. *Snap out of it!* she told herself. *He's here to protect me, not to be my friend. Definitely not to be my boyfriend.*

Feeling more in control of her emotions, she looked around the classroom. The two boys who'd been whispering had joined the group around Reed and were watching him intently. She stood up and walked over to see what was so fascinating.

He'd made a series of swans, large to small, and set them on the desk in front of him. There were also hearts and bunnies and boats. As she walked up, she heard one of the boys ask if he knew how to make an origami rose.

"My name's Tyler. My mom's been sick and when you made that tulip from paper yesterday, I wondered if you could make a rose so I could give to her." His voice trailed off, but his friend nudged him, encouraging him to explain. "She loves roses and I can't afford to buy her a real one, so . . ."

The other boy, Jason, handed Reed a square of shiny, red paper. "I found this in the art supply drawer. I thought it would make a pretty rose for Tyler's mom."

"I'd love to help you," Reed said, "on one condition."

"What's that?" Tyler's voice squeaked, his courage nearly failing him.

"I'll teach you, but you need to make it yourself." He gestured for Tyler to pull up a chair next to him, then he took a plain piece of paper and started folding it, explaining as he went. "I'll show you how to make a rose using this paper. Then you can practice and make a few on your own. Once you get this down, you can use the fancy paper and give that one to your ma."

Tyler's face lit up and he grabbed a piece of paper, ready to follow Reed's instructions.

"I'd like to try, too, if you don't mind," Jason piped in.

"Of course! Scoot in here." Reed made room and handed him a sheet of paper.

As she watched the three of them focus on the origami, their heads bent over the task, she felt a bit of shame. She'd thought these two boys were up to something when they were just trying to work up the courage to ask Reed to help them. She'd totally forgotten he'd filled the time yesterday doing origami, but apparently it had made an impression on the two boys. Her eyes filled with tears at the beauty of the moment, and she discretely wiped her eyes with the back of her finger.

She returned to the front of the classroom and sat at her desk, still feeling guilty for her suspicions. She saw Mary watching her, so she gestured for the girl to join her and grabbed a chair, setting it next to her desk. Mary was hesitant, but when Susan smiled, she thawed and took the seat.

"I'm sorry, Mary. I didn't mean to ruin the lesson today." Mary took her learning seriously, she wanted to get into a good college and move to a big city. She got upset when anything interfered with her lessons.

Mary shrugged her shoulders. "It's okay. I wasn't that into it either." She sighed and looked back at Reed, Tyler and Jason. "When is your brother going home?"

Startled, Susan looked at her student's face, but her expression was wide-open, and friendly. "I don't really know. I guess he'll be staying until he's ready to leave." *Great 'non-answer' answer, Susan.*

Mary's face wrinkled as she tried to decipher what Susan was saying. "I have no idea what that means, but it looks like the boys are enjoying his company."

She looked back and now there were five boys working on origami with Reed. She grinned and nodded. "It does indeed." She paused, then looked directly at the girl. "You don't seem to like Reed at all. May I ask why not?"

Mary chewed on her thumbnail; her face scrunched up in thought. "It's not that I don't like him, it's just . . . I don't think I can really trust any man right now." Her voice trailed off and she felt her heart constrict. After all this girl had been through, it made sense that she wouldn't trust Reed.

Feeling guilty again, this time for not realizing his presence was hard on her student, she bowed her head. "I'm sorry, Mary. It didn't occur to me that it might bother you to have him in the classroom. He's my brother and I can vouch for him being a good guy." She paused, but the girl's wary expression didn't change.

"I'm sorry if you're uncomfortable, but he's not going anywhere, at least right away, so if you'd like I can transfer you to Ms. Miller's class until he leaves."

Mary looked stricken and she quickly assured her she didn't want to be transferred. "No, Miss

Sinclair, it's okay. He seems nice and I'm fine with him being here. Really, it's fine."

She held back a grin. Mary had looked positively horrified at the thought of changing classes, even temporarily. But she'd have to keep an eye on her and if she determined it would be in the girl's best interest, she'd speak with the principal about a transfer. "Okay, then. You let me know if anything changes." Mary nodded just as the school bell rang, signaling the day was over.

IN THE TEACHER'S LOUNGE, Jenny was hunched over, her head in her hands. "What's up, Jenny?" Susan walked over and placed a hand on her friend's shoulder.

The woman raised her teary eyes up to meet hers. "Oh, you know me. My big mouth got away from me and I said some things to your brother that I didn't really mean. Then I got flustered and said some worse things. I've been worried that you won't want to be friends anymore."

Susan sat down next to the upset woman with a grin on her face. "Reed didn't tell me what was said, but I could see it upset him. He told me he'd made you angry and you might not want to be friends with me anymore, because of him."

Jenny gasped. "I never want to lose your friendship. I knew I was being dumb as the words tumbled out of my mouth, but by then it was too late to shove them back in." A single tear rolled down her face and she sniffled, miserably.

Susan took her friend's hand in hers. "Tell you what, next week you and I will have lunch together and you can tell me all about it." She started to stand up, then froze in place. "But for now, maybe you two shouldn't talk to each other. At least until you and I have a chance to clear the air." She finished standing and flexed her weary shoulders.

"You look like crap." Jenny immediately clamped her hand over her mouth and looked up at her, mortified. But Susan only laughed.

"I didn't get much sleep last night, so yeah, I look like crap." She caught sight of Reed standing outside the door. "Reed's here, so I gotta go." She started to walk towards the door but stopped suddenly at her friend's next words.

"When is he leaving, anyway?"

Jenny was wiping at her eyes with a napkin, so she couldn't see her expression. "Why?" Her heart was racing. Why had a student and a teacher both asked about Reed in the same day?

The woman tossed the napkin into the trash. "I just wondered if he'll be here for the Spring dance. I'll bet he's really good at the electric slide." She waggled her eyebrows at her, then pretended to fan herself.

"Jenny, you are a mess."

"I know, I know. But I'm a lovable mess. See you tomorrow. It's Friday, you know."

"Yes, I am aware," she said drily, shaking her head. She waved goodbye and walked out to meet Reed.

———

"EVERYTHING OKAY?" Reed asked as they walked to the car.

"Yeah. I told Jenny I'd have lunch with her next week so we can talk about whatever you two argued about."

"Good, I think that's a wise way to handle it. But you should eat *before* you talk because you'll probably lose your appetite."

She heard the anger in his voice and turned to look at him. She was distracted by movement behind him; someone ducked behind a tree near the school entrance. She put her hand on Reed's arm and leaned forward. "Don't be obvious, but I just saw someone hide behind the tree about 15 yards behind you."

He nodded and turned towards the car. He took a few steps, then dropped his keys. "Oh man, I'm so clumsy today." She started giggling at his dramatic announcement and tried to cover it with a fake cough.

As Reed bent to pick up his keys, he glanced back towards the school. He saw the toes of a brown shoe peeking out from behind a large oak tree, and his adrenaline kicked in. He looked at her and mouthed, "follow my lead." She nodded and together, they started walking to her car. Susan beeped the alarm and unlocked the driver's side door, then climbed in. As she inserted the key into the ignition, Reed smacked himself in the forehead.

"Oh man, I left my notepad in the classroom. I need to go back and get it." He opened the passenger door, slung his backpack into the passenger seat, leaned down and winked at her. He backed up and closed the car door, then took off at a full run towards the school building. When he got close to the tree, he made a sudden detour, heading straight at it.

"Ah ha!" he yelled. Susan watched from the car as he walked all the way around the tree, then knelt. He stood up and headed away from her, staring at the ground.

She was nervous when he disappeared from view, but after a few moments, he returned to the car, chuckling.

"It appears you witnessed a romantic tryst." He climbed in, his longs legs hitting the dashboard, a smile on his face. "There was no one there, but when I examined the ground, there were two sets of foot-prints, facing each other, and one set was slightly smaller than the other. I followed the prints to the student parking lot, but they ended at the pavement. I must have just missed them."

Susan sighed and rubbed her eyes. "I guess I'm starting to see threats everywhere," she told him. "I'm sorry for overreacting."

Reed looked at her, then reached out and placed his hand on her arm. "Never apologize for alerting me to something off. I'd much rather have a false alarm than have you hesitate to tell me something."

She looked into his eyes and knew he was telling her the truth. "I appreciate that. Thank you for protecting me and looking out for me." She grinned at the man seated next to her and he grinned back.

"Why, shucks, ma'am, just doing my job," he drawled.

She laughed. "Oh, Reed, you are a silly, silly man!" She started the car and drove towards home, while they argued about what to have for dinner.

9

THEY'D COMPROMISED on dinner and gone to the buffet. While Reed loaded his plate with steak, baked potato, veggies and salad, Susan opted for meatloaf, onion rings and mozzarella sticks.

"Really?" he asked for the third time.

"Yes, really. I'm hungry and I want comfort food. If this is too much for you, you'd better leave now," she warned. "I plan on having cake, ice cream and pie as my next course."

He watched as she took a bite of an onion ring, her eyes closing as she savored the greasy, breaded treat. He wished he could eat like that, but he knew that loading up on greasy food, no matter how yummy, could lead to a bellyache later. He'd stick to his vegetables, meat and potatoes, he decided. But it sure was fun to watch her enjoy her food!

He speared a chunk of iceberg lettuce, then a cherry tomato and topped it with a black olive. He dipped it into the cup of Italian dressing, then lifted it to his lips.

Susan nearly dropped her fork as his lips closed around the salad. She grabbed her ice water and took a long sip.

"You okay?" Reed thought maybe she'd bitten into a jalapeno because her face was bright red and she was sweating.

"I'm okay," Susan squeaked. She took another drink of water, then ducked her head and took a deep breath.

"You know, milk is better for killing the heat." He was trying to be helpful, but his advice made her face turn beet red and she retreated behind her glass of water once more.

"OH, my goodness, I ate too much," Susan whined on the ride home. She'd asked Reed to drive since she was feeling a little queasy.

He turned to look at her with one eyebrow lifted.

"What?" she asked, "Why are you looking at me like that?"

"Really? You're surprised you have a tummy ache?" he chuckled and turned back to the road. "You ate three desserts after having two plates of greasy, cheesy, calorie-laden food. And you wonder why you don't feel so hot."

"I do feel hot," she snapped, "I just don't feel-- good." She turned and glared at him.

He grinned and turned the car into the subdivision. They were about a block away from her home when he heard her moan. "Um, Reed, you might want to step on it."

He took one look at her pale face and realized she wasn't kidding. As he parked in her driveway, she started to get out of the car. He placed a hand on her arm and reminded her, "I know you're feeling sick, but I need to check it out first."

Susan nodded and grimaced, the movement apparently increasing her nausea. "I don't want to stay in the car, just in case. I'll just stand here by the side of the car until you whistle," she joked.

Reed walked to the porch, grinning. Anyone who could joke when they felt sick was a star in his book. The grin died on his face as he saw the bundle of herbs. This time, they were dried up, not fresh.

And underneath was a photo of him, with the eyes cut out.

"What the heck?" He spun around and found Susan standing on the bottom step of the porch, her eyes blazing and her hands on her hips. "This is not okay!"

He was annoyed with her for not waiting near the car, but right now, his first priority was to keep her safe. He grabbed her elbow and steered her into the house. He stopped just inside the door and pulled out his gun.

"Stay here and don't move," he told her. "I mean it, Susan." He glared at her until she lowered her eyes and nodded. Frustration made him move faster and he cleared the house in no time. He pulled out his phone and called Maggie as he walked back to where Susan was standing, staring out the door.

"We got another present," he said, his voice terse and raspy. "It's escalated again." He heard a noise and looked over to see Susan running for the bathroom. "And now Susan's throwing up her desserts, so, yeah."

"Is that some kind of weird euphemism?" Maggie chuckled.

He sighed and ran his hand over his face. "I wish. Susan's literally throwing up. Just come over as soon as you can and bring the crime scene techs. If we're lucky, the perp got sloppy and left us some fingerprints."

"Will do," Maggie said. "And Reed?"

"Yes, partner?"

"Bring her a cool, wet washcloth and a glass of ice water."

"Thanks, Maggie. See you soon."

———————

"WHAT IS WRONG WITH ME?" Susan whispered to herself as she rested, sitting on the floor next to the toilet. A soft knock at the door made her jump, and she felt her face flame red. "Yes?"

"Can I open the door?" Reed's deep voice sounded calm, but she knew he was worried about her.

She sighed. She'd have to see him eventually. She couldn't hide in the bathroom for the rest of her life. "Yes, Reed. Come on in."

He opened the door hesitantly, waiting until he saw her face to push it all the way open. "I'm not very good at this, but I brought you a cool, wet washcloth and some ice water."

As he stood there, awkward but adorable, her

heart melted the rest of the way. She'd never been in love before and had expected love to be blinding and breath-taking and jarring. But at this moment, she knew that she loved this man with all her heart and all she felt was happy, warm and secure. She didn't need fireworks, she needed Reed.

She smiled up at him and he grinned back. He handed her the water and clumsily fumbled with the wash cloth. "I'm not sure, am I supposed to place this on your head or your neck or just hand it to you."

She took a small sip of water to rinse her mouth, then reached for the cloth. She folded it and placed it on the back of her neck. "Thank you, that feels good." She closed her eyes for a moment, enjoying the cooling sensation.

She could hear him shuffle from one foot to the other, so she opened her eyes and looked up at him. "I didn't know how to help, so I asked Maggie."

"It's okay, Reed. I appreciate it no matter who thought of it." She sighed. "I'm so sorry."

He plopped down on the floor next to her and smiled gently. She wanted to take his hand, but she had a glass of water in one and the other was holding the cloth to her neck.

"You have nothing to apologize for. You've been through so much recently and had to do it all alone.

I'm a trained U.S. Marshal and this stuff is freaking *me* out." He rubbed the back of his neck with his hand. "I'm really impressed with how well you've been coping. Even if you didn't listen when I told you not to eat the pie after the cake," he grinned.

Susan giggled and looked sideways at him. "I didn't really have a choice," she confessed. "About the coping, not the pie and the cake." He grinned at her clarification. "It was either cope or give up; and for me, giving up was not an option."

"Don't sell yourself short," he argued. "I've seen people in WITSEC withdraw into depression or anger. They couldn't bounce back from what they'd experienced, and they withdrew into themselves. If I didn't know your story, I would have no idea that you'd been through any kind of trauma, let alone witnessing a murder, having to relocate and all."

They sat there in silence for a few moments, lost in their own thoughts. That ended when there was a loud knock at the front door, then Maggie's voice shouting, "Is it safe to enter?"

He grinned at her and she could feel her cheeks turn pink in embarrassment. He called out to Maggie as he stood up, then he turned and held out his hand to help her up.

Once on her feet, she asked for a moment of

privacy to clean up and Reed nodded, pulling the door closed behind him.

Susan looked at herself in the mirror. Her hair was all mussed and her mascara had run, making her look like a raccoon. She grimaced at her reflection. She ran the washcloth under hot water then wiped away the mascara mess. She brushed her teeth and her hair and braced herself to face Maggie. Reed had been polite, even when he teased her. But she knew his partner wasn't going to let her off that easy.

10

MAGGIE WAS SQUATTED DOWN, staring grimly at the photo and bundle of herbs. Reed stopped next to her on the porch. "Thanks for getting here so fast, and for the washcloth and water advice."

She grunted and ran her hand down her face. "This isn't good, Reed. It isn't good at all. The perp is escalating, changing the pattern and I can't for the life of me figure out why." She paused and stood up, placing her hands on her hips. "This doesn't feel like the New York threat. Susan was right, it feels personal and angry."

"Right? This feels emotional and Bruno doesn't have feelings," Susan piped up from behind him.

He turned to look at her. She'd washed her face, so the black mascara smudges were gone, and she'd changed her clothes. She looked fresh and clean and somehow even more vulnerable. He swallowed hard and renewed his determination to keep her safe.

Maggie, on the other hand, didn't seem impressed by her transformation. Her brow furrowed and a frown appeared on her face. "What were you thinking, Susan?"

Susan bowed her head and nodded. "I know, I know. I screwed up and Reed had to take care of me instead of doing his job." She looked up at the woman's disapproving glare and squared her shoulders. "I take full responsibility for my actions today. I'm sorry and it won't happen again."

Reed was confused by his partner's tone and Susan's response. He started to defend Susan but one look at Maggie's face and he realized that there was more going on here.

"I realize that this has been tough on you," Maggie began. "But you made this decision and promised to follow the rules. One of those rules is to keep a low profile and let us do our jobs. Reed was so worried about you that he left the porch unattended. Luckily it doesn't appear that anyone tampered with anything. But that doesn't absolve you."

He couldn't take it anymore. He had to stand up for her. "Come on Maggie, she didn't do anything wrong or on purpose. She just ate too much, that's all. It isn't a big deal."

He was surprised when Susan turned to him, tears in her eyes, shaking her head, no.

"Reed, it wasn't a random thing. When I was younger, I suffered from bulimia. It took a lot of therapy and time to undo those bad habits, but I overcame them. I learned to enjoy food and eating and not to use it to numb myself. Today, I slipped up. I was tired of being in control all the time. I was tired of being afraid. Even though I didn't set out to eat too much and make myself sick, there was a part of me that knew what I was doing." She looked up at him and he could see in her eyes that she was begging him for forgiveness.

He was torn. Why hadn't either of them told him about this? Was he always going to be kept out of the loop? He'd been given this assignment at the last minute and had spooked the witness because he didn't know the details of her situation. Now this had happened. If he'd known about the bulimia, he might have realized what was happening and kept her from eating too much. Didn't his partner trust him enough to share information with him? What the heck?

He knew getting angry wasn't going to solve anything, but he was already there. He felt himself clench and unclench his fists while he looked from Susan's face to his sister-in-law's face and back again.

Unable to formulate words to express his frustration and hurt feelings, he grunted and turned around, heading through the house for the back yard. He heard Susan's gasp then Maggie's soft voice. "Let him go."

REED HEARD footsteps coming up the path and he looked up into Maggie's concerned face. She sat down on the bench next to him and they sat in silence for a few minutes. Reed was irritated and unhappy, but this was his partner and his sister-in-law. He decided to wait and let her explain herself, rather than accuse her and potentially make things worse.

She reached over and grabbed his hand, holding it with hers. She cleared her throat and started talking. "I know you're upset with me right now, but I didn't purposely keep this from you," she told him. "The bulimia wasn't part of the case file and I only know about it because Susan shared it with me when we relocated her. Even Jackson didn't know."

Hearing that made him feel a little better, and he

squeezed her hand to let her know he was listening. "I'm sure you haven't shared everything you've learned about Susan with me, either. It's not possible to document every single word and every detail of every conversation. Even if we are trained U.S. Marshals." She chuckled, and he grinned in spite of himself.

"What she shared with me was a private moment and I had no idea it would come back to bite me. I don't think she realized what was happening either, or she would have shared it with you, herself." She let go of his hand and turned to face him. "I need you to put aside your hurt feelings and help me here, Reed," she pleaded.

"My being here has agitated the perp and it hasn't gotten us any closer to figuring out who that is." He looked at his partner hoping she'd disagree, but her guarded expression showed she'd reached the same conclusion.

"I think I should stay here with Susan and you should take a break." Reed felt his anger rise at her words, but she held up her hand to stop him before he could argue. "Just hear me out. You've been on duty for several days, 24 hours a day. Just take a day off, relax, get some rest. We can meet here tomorrow at this time and discuss what we want to do next."

She reached into her pocket and handed him her car keys.

He wanted to tell her just what he thought of her plan, but Susan appeared at the back door, and he looked up into her stricken face. "Why does Reed have to leave?" she asked, her voice trembling. He looked at Maggie's determined face and even though the thought of being away from Susan made his heart hurt, he knew it was the right thing to do. He took the car keys from his partner's hand, stood up and walked over to her.

"She's right, Susan. It's better if she stays here tonight and tomorrow. Hopefully that will deescalate things on this end and it'll give me a chance to relax, so I can think straight." He paused; his expression thoughtful. He leaned forward and whispered, "remember when we talked about needing space?" He watched her expression lighten as she remembered, and instantly felt bad. He hated misleading her, even if it was to keep her safe.

"I don't want you to leave, but I respect your need for a little alone time." Her eyes were wide, and her voice was wobbly, but she lifted her chin and did her best to smile at him.

Reed wanted to pull her into his arms and never let her go, but since he couldn't do that, he muttered a gruff good night to the two women and headed for the car.

He was still hurt and angry and he found himself speeding through the neighborhood. A small child standing on the sidewalk alone gave Reed pause, and he slowed down to check it out. About three feet behind the child was a very pregnant woman. As Reed drove slowly past, he heard her call the child to come sit with her on the grass. The child smiled and waved at Reed, then toddled back to his mother, who gathered him in her arms and kissed him on the forehead.

Reed sobered up quickly, realizing that his anger served no good purpose. He pulled the car over and turned off the engine. Why was he so angry? What was going on with him? He knew Maggie well enough to know that she'd never purposely keep information from him. He was usually a good judge of character and his gut was telling him that Susan was honest, and he could trust her. So why was he getting so upset?

He hated to admit it, but he was angry at himself, not at the two women. He was developing feelings for Susan. Rule 1 of being a U.S. Marshal: do not get personally attached to the witness. He slammed his hands down on the steering wheel.

This was his first major case and he was mucking it up.

He took a deep breath and ran his hands through his hair. He needed to put his feelings aside and do his job. He was a U.S. Marshal and he was going to protect his witness. He looked at himself in the rearview mirror and saw the determination on his face.

Decision made, Reed started the car and pulled away from the curb. A plan was formulating in his mind and as he drove, he made a mental list of things he'd need to get the job done.

HAVING Maggie around was definitely different than having Reed around. The woman wanted to talk all the time and she didn't cook. Two hours in and Susan was in desperate need of some alone time.

"I'm really tired, Maggie," Susan said, yawning widely for effect. "I think I'm going to turn in now."

Maggie smiled at her witness. "It is getting late. I'm going to take a look around outside then I'll turn in as well," she announced.

Susan nodded and walked to her bedroom. She closed the door behind her and sighed. It had been a long day and she really was tired. But she was also confused. She'd been worried about having Reed stay here, and it had been a breeze. Having Maggie here was a whole different story. She wasn't sure she wanted to examine why too closely.

She washed up and got ready for bed. When she heard Maggie return, closing the front door behind her and locking it, she turned off her light and crawled into bed.

"All clear, good night," she called out from the hallway.

"Thanks Maggie," she replied. "Good night."

She closed her eyes and placed her palms together. She said her prayers, then snuggled into her bed, hoping for a good night's sleep. But the image of distraught blue eyes played across the inside of her eyelids until slumber finally overtook her.

OUTSIDE, Reed watched as the lights went out in Susan's bedroom and then in the guest room. He was standing in the shadow of a large Texas Ash across the street from her house. He stayed put for 15 minutes, waiting to see if anything happened. Everything stayed quiet, so he walked back to where he'd parked his car.

He'd noticed the neighbor who lived three doors down and across the street from Susan worked graveyard, so he knew driveway would be empty all night. He'd backed in, making sure he had a clear line of sight to her house. He'd dressed in black jeans, black T-shirt and black jacket, which helped him blend into the shadows. Inside the car he had bottled water, snacks and earbuds, so he could listen to music while he kept watch. He planned to get out and walk around every 30 minutes, hoping he could catch the perp in the act.

He knew Maggie would be angry with him for not listening to her, but he also knew he wasn't the type of person who quit in the middle of a job. And he was a grown man, he didn't need a time out from his sister-in-law. He jumped when his phone vibrated, grinning when he saw the caller ID.

"Hey Maggie, I was nearly asleep. Is everything okay?" He yawned, hoping she'd believe he was home in bed.

"Cut the act, partner. I saw you across the street when I patrolled and I'm pretty sure that right now you're sitting in your car three houses down," Maggie told him. Before he could come up with an excuse, she added, "Thank you, Reed. I'll sleep better knowing you're out there."

The phone disconnected and he grinned in the dark. He was a lucky man to have such an amazing partner and sister-in-law. Even if she was a pain in the neck sometimes.

11

REED STAYED ALERT ALL NIGHT, watching and waiting. He made his rounds every 30 minutes, but never saw anything out of place. It was 5:30 am and still no sign of the perp when the light came on in the guest room and his phone vibrated.

"Good morning, Maggie."

"If you say so." She sounded tired and cranky and he grinned to himself. "Did you solve the case while I slept on a lumpy mattress?"

"Nope. Nothing happened. Not a single thing." He heard her sigh of frustration and wished he had better news.

"Well, go home and get some sleep. You're back on witness duty tonight. I can't handle another night in that bed." She groaned and added, "The mattress did a number on my back and I can't sleep without my husband's snoring. I'll call you later."

His heart leapt into his throat and he was glad she'd hung up. He wouldn't have been able to speak; he was so relieved. He started the car and drove home, thrilled that his partner still trusted him and excited about seeing Susan again.

SUSAN WOKE up to a strange flopping noise outside her bedroom door. Still half-asleep, fear made her heart beat faster and she pulled the blankets up to her chin. A groan and a muttered, "Oh, my aching back," reminded her that Maggie had stayed the night, and was now walking around in her floppy bunny slippers, which explained the strange noise.

She sat up and swung her legs over the side of the bed. There was no smell of coffee or bacon to entice her to get up, so she dawdled for a moment, wondering where Reed was and if he was making breakfast for himself--or someone else.

She was instantly irritated by where her thoughts had taken her, and she wondered again how he'd managed to get under her skin so fast. A knock sounded at the door and Maggie peeked her head in.

"I need caffeine, desperately," she groaned. "And I can't figure out how to operate your danged coffee maker."

Susan grinned at the disheveled woman at her door, no longer the put together U.S. Marshal who could handle anything. "Okay, give me just a minute and I'll make us some coffee and eggs," she replied.

"Bless you," Maggie gushed as she pulled the door shut.

Susan paused to say a morning prayer, thanking the Lord for keeping her safe overnight and asking for patience in dealing with Maggie. She threw on a robe and headed for the kitchen to start the coffee.

"WHERE'S REED?" Brenda's husky, nasal voice assaulted her ears as she and Maggie walked into the teacher's lounge to get a cup of coffee.

"Good morning to you, too." She wasn't in the mood to deal with the woman, but she turned and gestured towards the marshal. "Brenda this is Maggie, she's a friend of mine and she's helping today while Reed takes care of some business.

Maggie, this is Brenda." She headed for the coffee pot and left the two women to fend for themselves.

Brenda sniffed as her gaze traveled up and down Maggie, who stared back at the women without flinching. "I like Reed better." She lifted her coffee mug up to her lips and was mid-sip when Maggie responded.

"I like Reed better than you, too." She turned on her heel and left, leaving Susan to deal with a sputtering Brenda.

"Well, I never!" The woman's face was angry and red as she grabbed a napkin and wiped at the coffee she'd sprayed onto her shirt.

She had no sympathy for her. "You were rude first." She grabbed the paperwork from her cubby and followed Maggie out the door, ignoring the woman's glare.

Outside in the hall, the marshal waited for her, one foot propped up on a bench. "I'm sorry, but she's about half a brick short of a load and she made my teeth itch."

She laughed, shaking her head. "I have no idea what that means, but I'm pretty sure I agree." She led the way to her classroom and held the door for Maggie to enter. As the two women walked in, Tyler ran over to them holding a perfect origami rose.

"I did it, Miss Sinclair!" He looked at Maggie, then behind her, then he looked at Susan. "Where's Reed? He was supposed to help me make a rose with the fancy paper."

"I'm so sorry, Tyler! Reed got called away on business. This is my friend, Maggie. She's helping out today." His face fell and her heart plummeted with it.

"Well, that is one mighty fine paper rose, if I do say so myself," Maggie drawled, drawing the boy's attention to her. "Reed will be back tomorrow and I'm sure he'll be glad to help you make your fancy one. But I wonder, do you think you could show me how to make one of these?"

"Well, I'm still learning, but I'd be glad to show you what I know." Tyler motioned for her to follow him to his desk and Maggie winked at Susan as she walked away.

She wasn't sure which startled her most: Maggie's thick, fake accent or her announcement about Reed. She grinned and shook her head: never underestimate a U.S. marshal.

IT WAS NEARLY the end of the day when Susan

remembered her meeting with Mary. She'd noticed the girl seemed especially happy today and she was curious to find out why. On the last break of the day, while eating donuts in the teacher's lounge, she told Maggie they'd need to stay late.

"Oh no!" The marshal was obviously distressed. "I scheduled an appointment with my doctor for right after class. I planned to drop you off at the office for safekeeping until I was done." Her face had gone beet red and Susan was intrigued.

"What kind of doctor's appointment?" she teased, not really expecting an answer, since it was none of her business.

Maggie looked around, then twirled a strand of hair around her fingers. She sighed and looked at Susan. "I'm not sure. I've been feeling a little queasy and this morning when I couldn't figure out how to make coffee, I realized I've also been experiencing some brain fog. I called my doctor while you were in class and he said he wanted to see me right away." She looked at Susan, her expression full of wonder and a bit of fear. "He thinks I'm pregnant."

"Oh, Maggie, that's wonderful!" Susan clapped her hands and grinned at the marshal.

"I can't leave you alone, so I'll just reschedule the appointment. It's no big deal."

"No, you won't!" she said, her voice stern. "I'll be here at the school and I promise I won't go anywhere until you get back. You just go take care of business and don't worry about me!"

She looked uncertain but nodded. "I'll think about it. Meanwhile, our break is over. I'll walk you to class then I need to stop by the ladies' room. I'll join you in the classroom when I'm done," she said.

"Oh, I'm so excited for you," Susan gushed. "And nervous, too. And jealous."

Maggie's face flamed and she ducked her head. "Just get to class, missy, before the tardy bell rings and you get sent to detention."

Susan walked into the classroom, happy for her friend, a big grin on her face.

REED PICKED up the ringing phone. "I thought you told me to get some sleep," he muttered.

"Can it, Reed," his sassy partner told him. "Change in plans."

He listened to Maggie as she explained what she wanted him to do.

"Got it! I'll be there." He hung up feeling like a load had been lifted from his shoulders. She'd asked him to take over watching Susan this afternoon.

She trusts me after all, he thought. And he was going to see Susan! He headed for the shower, whistling as he walked.

12

"OKAY, Mary, I have to ask, why are you so happy today?" She scooted over so Mary could sit next to her at the desk.

"Well, I guess . . . oh, there isn't really a reason," Mary told her. "It's just a beautiful day today!"

Susan was still curious, but with the distractions of Maggie's potential pregnancy and Reed's return, she didn't push too hard. "Well, okay, then. Are you ready to work on that essay?"

Mary handed her two photos. "I think I might want to use one of these instead of the seven we chose last time. I'm just not sure. Will you look at them with me and help me decide?"

"Absolutely." She looked at the two photos and was impressed. "These look amazing, Mary! I approve of your choices 100%. All of your photos are outstanding, but these two are extra special."

She looked up to see a blush stain the girl's cheeks. Mary's smile was huge, and she grinned back, glad to see her so happy. She grabbed a pen and a pad of paper and they began brainstorming what to say in the essay.

REED PEEKED through the small window in the classroom door and was relieved to see that everything was okay. He'd met up with Maggie a few moments ago and she'd told him to let Susan know he was here.

Two startled sets of eyes looked up at him as he opened the classroom door. One set lit up and the other set immediately looked away. He grinned into Susan's surprised face and declared, "I'm back!"

She stood up and walked towards him. "Reed, what are you doing here? I thought you wouldn't be back until tomorrow."

"I finished my meetings early and headed back. I hope I'm not interrupting anything," he said, looking over her shoulder towards Mary.

The girl stood up and started packing her backpack. Susan looked at her student then turned back to him with concern in her eyes.

"Hi Mary." He frowned when Mary ignored him. He looked down at Susan who shrugged, then walked over to the girl.

"Mary?" She placed a hand on Mary's shoulder and leaned towards her. "We can still finish up," she said. "Why are you packing everything?"

Eyes full of tears turned towards Susan, then glanced over at him. "It's okay, we got a lot done. I know you prefer to spend time with him."

"I love spending time with you, too. Reed can wait until we're done." Susan placed her arms around Mary and gave her a hug.

Reed's blood ran cold when the girl suddenly looked up at him, meeting his eyes. The look she gave him made it clear they were enemies, and the prize was Susan.

Mary broke eye contact with him and stepped back from Susan. "It's okay, really," she told her teacher. "Once he's gone, things will be back to normal." She smiled at Susan and walked out of the classroom without looking in his direction at all.

Susan walked over to him, a tentative smile on her face. "That was weird," she said. She looked up at Reed, her eyes shining, and his heart lodged in his throat. "Hi. I missed you."

Confused by the intensity of his response to her, he reminded himself he was a U.S. Marshal with a job to do. He stepped back to put a little distance between them. "Of course, you missed me. You missed my fine coffee and my amazing cooking!"

Her brow furrowed for a moment, but she quickly followed his lead. "Yep, that's it. Maggie didn't cook and she couldn't even figure out how to use the coffee maker. Now that you mention it, I'm starving!" She grinned, but Reed could see she was hurt and confused.

He sighed and rubbed his hand over his chin. "I need to talk with you for a minute. Let's have a seat." She sat at the desk and he sat in the chair that Mary had vacated.

"I am a U.S. Marshal charged with protecting you." He grabbed her hand and held it in his as he watched conflicting emotions pass across her face.

"I know that, Reed. What are you trying to say?"

"I'm trying to say that I like you. I really like you. As a woman, not just a witness. But keeping you safe is the most important thing, so I need to put a little distance between us, even though I'd rather get closer."

Susan's face turned a lovely shade of pink and she looked like she was about to cry. But she didn't cry. She stuck out her chin, looked him in the eye and said what was on her mind. "I appreciate that, and I'm sorry if I've been making your job difficult. But when this is over, I expect you to take me on a real date and then we'll just see what happens."

Reed's heart started pounding in his chest and he wished things were different. He'd seen Susan's fear and her loneliness, and he'd seen her courage. She was an amazing woman he'd be proud to have in his life. But for now, she was his witness and he wasn't going to let her down.

He nodded and let go of her hand. Switching to official U.S. Marshal mode, he said, "Tell me what you know about Mary."

"Why?" Susan's brow creased again.

"She gave me a look that told me to back off. She made it clear you're her property."

"Oh that," she waved her hand in the air. "She's just lonely and I'm the only adult in her life that she feels she can trust."

"Still, I got a strange vibe from her today and my gut is telling me to keep an eye on her."

"I respect that," she said. "I'll tell you what I know on the way back to my place. Or did you want to stop and get dinner?" As soon as the words were out of her mouth, she paled, and her mouth dropped open. "I'm sorry, Reed. The last time was a fluke. It won't happen again, I promise."

He placed his hand on her shoulder to reassure her, but quickly pulled it back and tucked it into the front pocket of his jeans. "Actually, I picked up some groceries so I could make you a home-cooked meal, if that's alright with you."

"That sounds wonderful!" She started packing up her belongings and Reed was watching her when a movement outside the door startled him. He jumped up, instantly alert.

"What is it?" Susan asked, her voice quiet.

"I'm not sure. I thought I saw someone looking in the door." He walked to the door and threw it open, looking up and down the hallway, but there was no one there. He was confident he'd seen something, but he didn't want to upset her, so he turned around with a shrug. "False alarm, I guess."

"Good. I'm ready to go home." They walked out to the parking lot and didn't see anyone or anything suspicious, but Reed's senses were still on high alert. He knew he'd seen something, and his gut was telling him to be extra careful.

SUSAN PONDERED Mary's behavior as Reed drove them back to her home. The girl had always been a little twitchy, but today her reaction had been extreme. Something was definitely going on with the girl, but she was at a loss as to what it could be.

She looked over at Reed and marveled at how different it felt to have him sitting next to her rather than Maggie. Or anyone else for that matter. She'd never felt as safe and as cherished as she did with Reed. He had his U.S. Marshal persona firmly in place, and she was grateful he'd allowed her to see the man behind the professional.

She appreciated what he'd said back at the school. Even though they both had feelings, this wasn't the time to explore them. They needed to focus on solving this mystery and once it was over, God willing, they'd be able to see if there was a future for the two of them. For now, she'd relax and trust they'd keep her safe. But it was hard with him sitting so close--with his big silver belt buckle, his muscles and his gorgeous smile.

She was so caught up in her thoughts she didn't realize she'd chuckled out loud until Reed turned to her, one eyebrow raised. She just shrugged her shoulders. She couldn't share her thoughts with him right now, and that was okay. She smiled out the window and enjoyed the rest of the drive home.

REED COULD SENSE she was deep in thought, but when she burst out laughing, he turned and saw a blush on her cheeks and a sparkle in her eyes. She didn't share what was funny, but the look in her eyes made his stomach do flip flops. He turned his eyes back to the road and focused on doing his job.

When they reached the house, he didn't have to say anything. "I know the drill," she said, grinning to show she wasn't irritated. "I'll sit here and wait for you to check the porch, then when you whistle, I'll come running."

He knew she was teasing, and he had to join in. "One whistle for 'all clear' and two for 'run for the hills'?" he asked, waggling his eyebrows. He'd expected to her to laugh or tell him he hadn't learned his lesson, but she just gazed into his eyes and for a moment, he stopped breathing.

Reed shook his head to clear his mind and get back to business. He saw the grin on Susan's face as she turned to look out the window, and he wondered if his feelings were written all over his face.

He got out of the car, his eyes scanning the yard and the neighborhood as he walked. He had one foot on the bottom step when he saw it. A photo of him and Susan, with a big hole cut into his chest. He grabbed his phone and dialed Maggie, signaling for Susan to stay in the car.

"Hey Maggie, another gift, another escalation." His somber tone conveyed his concern and she responded instantly.

"I'm still at the doctor's office, but I'll send the crime scene unit and some patrol cars. I'll be there as soon as I can."

The gasp next to him didn't entirely surprise him. He hadn't really expected Susan to stay in the car and follow his directions, but he wished she had.

"Hey, are you alright to stay here for a moment?" he asked. He needed to check out the house so he could get her inside, but after last time, he wasn't willing to leave the porch unattended.

Her face was pale and pinched, but she nodded vigorously and told him to hurry. He bounded up the steps, leaving the door wide open so he could hear her call if she needed him. He cleared the house and returned to the front door.

She was sitting on the top step, about 16 inches from the offending picture, looking out into the front yard. He walked over and sat down next to her. She turned to look him and tried to smile, but her lips just quivered as tears ran down her face. Reed reached out and grabbed her hand, holding it tightly. They sat in silence while he tried to think of something comforting to say.

Susan drew a deep breath, took her hand back and wiped her face. She looked over at him and grinned. "I'm okay now but I'm hungry. What's for dinner?" This time her smile was genuine, and he smiled back at her. He stood up and held out his hand, helping her to feet. They carefully walked around the offensive "gift" and entered the house.

Reed hesitated, but Susan was one step ahead of him. She grabbed a chair from the kitchen and moved it into the hallway. "It's okay, leave the door open until the police get here. I'll keep an eye on things while you cook." She sat down in the chair and folded her arms across her chest. He grinned. Nobody better mess with *his* lady.

———

"OH, MY GOODNESS!" Susan moaned, rubbing

her tummy. "Another amazing meal, Mr. U.S. Marshal."

"Why thank you, Miss WITSEC witness."

Susan stood up and started placing dirty dishes in the sink. "I'll get to these in a few minutes," she said. "Right now, I'm too full to stand up."

Susan watched as pleasure and concern chased each other across his face. She walked over to him and looked him in the eye.

"This is why I don't talk about my bulimia. People who know about it watch everything I eat and check on me afterwards to make sure I'm not sneaking off to throw up." She grimaced and shrugged her shoulders. "I liked it better when you didn't know. Then you were happy when I ate with gusto."

Reed looked at her, his expression thoughtful. "I guess I'm just not sure how it works. When you say you're too full is that because you enjoyed the food or because you feel like you need to purge?" He shrugged his shoulders and raised his hands. "I looked it up, but I really don't understand."

Susan grinned. This handsome man had done some research. Knowing that he cared enough to google her illness made her feel tingly inside. *But now is not the time*, she told herself.

"How about we figure out what the heck is going on first, then I'll answer any questions you have about bulimia. For now, just know that I'm rubbing my belly because your carne asada tacos were divine and I enjoyed them immensely."

"Got it," Reed said. "Changing the subject to something I'm more comfortable with, do you mind if I use your laptop to do some research on Mary?"

Susan didn't believe it was Mary terrorizing them, but the girl's behavior today had been decidedly odd, so she nodded her head. "Go for it. I'm going to go sit on the porch for a few minutes and get some air." She held up her hand to stop him before he could argue with her. "The techs are still out there as well as two police officers. I'm sure I'll be fine."

She walked over to the front door and opened it, pausing for a moment. The techs had removed the picture and the dried-up rosemary, but the memory was still imprinted in Susan's mind. She sat down on the top step and watched the activity in her yard.

The police officers were interviewing her neighbor from across the street. Susan lifted her hand as the man waved at her, a big smile on his face. This was the most excitement this neighborhood had seen, and he was clearly enjoying the attention.

The techs were loading the last of their things into the truck and talking amongst themselves. They were almost done packing up so pretty soon, she and Reed would be alone again.

Susan leaned her head against the handrailing and closed her eyes. "Please God, let this be over soon. I'm so very tired," she prayed. She sat like that for a few moments, eyes closed, enjoying the sense of peace that came over her. Feeling renewed, she opened her eyes and stood up. Time to do the dishes.

13

REED FELT SICK. How was he going to tell Susan? He closed his eyes, but the disturbing images didn't disappear. He picked up his phone and dialed Maggie. The call went to voicemail, so he left her a terse message, "Hey Maggie. Check out Mary Garza's social media. We need to locate her right away. And where the heck are you? Call me back."

He looked up at Susan. She was washing the dishes, humming to herself. He hated to interrupt her, but she needed to know what he'd found.

"Hey Susan?" he called out.

"Yes, Reed?" Susan's sweet voice made his gut churn thinking about what he had to show her. He knew it would devastate her; but he had no choice.

"I've found something you need to see." He tried

not to sound freaked out, but the look on Susan's face as she walked towards him, drying her hands on a dish towel, told him he hadn't succeeded.

Susan stood behind him so she could view the laptop screen over his shoulder. When she realized what she was looking at, she gasped and grabbed Reed's shoulders, her fingers digging in as she struggled to come to terms with the images. "What the heck?" she whispered.

The screen was full of pictures and drawings of Susan. She leaned in closer, focused on the images on the screen. There were photos of her in the classroom, walking to her car, even photos of her in her own yard, weeding the garden. "Where she did get all those pictures of me? She must have been taking them in class and following me around for weeks. How did she find out where I live?"

Her voice was shaky, and Reed turned to look up at her, afraid she was going to fall apart. But her eyes were full of fury and her lips were twisted into a look of determination. "We need to find her and talk to her. This young woman needs help and she has some serious explaining to do."

Reed's phone dinged announcing a new text message. "It's Maggie. She says she's looking for Mary and will let us know when she finds her."

"I can't believe this." Susan's voice trembled and her eyes filled with tears. "I saw potential in Mary so I reached out to her. I'd lost everything too, even if it was in a different way. I thought I was doing a good thing." She looked down at Reed, seeking some kind of reassurance, but he didn't know what to say. He turned in the chair and took her hand in his.

"This girl was broken before you even met her," he said softly. "Befriending her wasn't a mistake. You probably gave her the most security and affection she's ever had in her life."

Susan reached for a napkin from the table and used it to wipe her eyes. "But how do you know I didn't make it worse for her?"

"You didn't make it worse for me, he did." Mary's voice came from behind them, startling them both. Susan jumped and Reed reached for his gun.

"Don't even think about it." Mary walked over to the table, keeping them both in her sights, holding a pistol firmly with both hands. "I saw you at the car that day, when you reached into your jacket and pulled out your gun. I promise, I'll shoot her if you try anything." Reed raised his hands above his head, and she nodded, "Good boy. Miss Sinclair, I need you to reach around and remove his gun, then toss it to me."

"Mary, let's just talk about this." Susan tried to start a conversation, but Mary pointed the gun at her head and her voice trailed off. She looked down at Reed who nodded. She leaned forward and reached into his jacket, pulling the gun from its holster. Holding it with two fingers, as if she couldn't bear to touch it, she set the gun on the table in front of Mary.

"That's a good girl," Mary crooned. She shifted the pistol to her right hand and used her left to take Reed's gun and throw it behind her, onto the floor.

Reed's mind was racing. He had to play this smart or they could both end up dead. He wasn't going to let that happen; not when he'd finally found the woman he wanted to marry. The realization hit him like a ton of bricks and for a moment, it took his breath away. He loved Susan and with her, he could have everything he'd ever wanted. He wasn't going to allow this girl to take away their future.

He took a deep breath. *Here goes nothing.* He looked down at the laptop screen. "So, Mary. This is a pretty cool site you have here. Did you take all these pictures yourself?"

"Shut up, Reed." Mary pointed the gun at his chest and Susan gasped.

"I'm sorry, Mary. I'll be quiet." *Well, that didn't work the way I'd hoped.*

Susan's hands gripped his shoulders and he could feel her shaking. "Mary, I don't understand. Why are you doing this?" Her voice was strong, but he could hear an undercurrent of panic and he prayed that she could hold it together a little longer.

"Why am I doing this?" Mary's voice was loud and full of fury. "Because you betrayed me, that's why. You betrayed me, just like everyone else I've ever loved. And you're both going to pay for it." She shifted her gun from hand to hand and aimed it first at Susan, then at Reed, then back at Susan.

He didn't want to antagonize the young woman, but he knew the longer he could keep her talking the better their chances of surviving. "You know, Mary, Susan really does care about you," he said softly.

The girl's eyes darted to Susan, widening as she nodded. "I really do. I have ever since I met you. I don't know what I did to upset you, but I'm so sorry."

Mary harsh laugh sounded more like a snort of derision and Reed felt Susan's fingers dig deeper into his shoulders. "You don't know what you did to upset me? How about abandoning me. How about lying to me and leaving me alone after you promised you'd always be there to protect me?"

Reed sensed a shift in the girl. Her pupils had dilated, and she seemed less focused, more unbalanced. She didn't seem to be talking about Susan anymore. He guessed she was talking about her mother.

Susan swallowed hard behind him. She let go of his shoulders and took a step towards Mary, her hands hanging loosely at her sides.

"I don't understand, Mary. What did I promise to protect you from?" Her voice sounded calm, but he heard a slight quiver. He wasn't sure if it was fear or anger, but he silently warned her to tread carefully.

"You know," Mary sniveled. "From him! You promised! And then you left me, and I was all alone."

Susan took another step towards Mary, her hands out, palms open. Mary's hand shook and the gun dipped, but she quickly lifted it, pointing at Reed. "Don't move again or I'll shoot him," she warned.

Susan stopped and he could see she was shaking like a leaf. "I'm sorry, Mary. I'm sorry if I let you down once, but I won't do it again. Just give me another chance." As she pleaded with the girl, she took another step and a shot rang out.

Reed felt a searing pain in his shoulder, and he was thrown against the back of the chair. He looked up into Susan's horrified eyes as he lifted his hand to his chest. He heard her say his name, but her voice sounded like it was underwater. Everything went blurry as he struggled to stay conscious.

"I told you not to move," Mary said, smugly. "I told you not to move then and I told you not to move now."

SUSAN WAS FURIOUS. She grabbed some napkins and pressed them into Reed's shoulder. She didn't like the vacant look in his eyes, but she wasn't in a position to do anything besides slow the bleeding. She knew she had to keep the girl talking if she wanted to keep Reed alive, so she asked, "What do you mean you told me not to move then?"

Reed grunted as she pressed the napkins into his wound, but the pain seemed to clear his head. Susan saw his eyes focus on her face and he managed a small nod, to let her know he was back. She winked at him, willing him to be strong, then turned to face her student.

"I asked you a question. What do you mean you told me not to move 'then'?" She placed her hands on her hips and she was pretty sure the girl could see the fire in her eyes. She was tired of being terrorized by a child and it was her fault Reed had been shot. She needed to get Mary to back down so she could get Reed to a hospital.

Mary's face crumpled and tears filled her eyes. "I didn't mean to do it. Really, I didn't. He'd already hit me twice and you hadn't done anything to stop him. I couldn't take any more. I told you to stand up to him or else. When you told me to put the gun down, I knew you'd always take his side. Then you started walking towards me. I told you to stop, but you didn't. I had to do it. I had to."

"Well, hello, Susan."

Susan closed her eyes and clenched her fists so hard she drew blood with her finger nails. This could not be happening. How were all of these people getting into her house. She needed to get a dog. A big dog. A big, scary dog with sharp teeth.

She opened her eyes and slowly turned to look at the man who'd just spoken--the man who'd committed murder in front of her. The man who wanted her dead.

BRUNO DELUCA WAS POINTING a gun at Susan. He was flanked by two large men, each the size of a small SUV, holding semi-automatic rifles aimed at Mary.

"You might want to tell your crazy friend here to put down her gun. You know firsthand that I have no problem dispatching. . . annoyances." The man's voice sounded rough, like sandpaper, and dripped with menace. Susan had hoped she'd never hear that voice again, outside of a courtroom. He waved his gun towards Mary. "Do it now or your friend here won't be the only one sporting a bullet hole."

She looked over at Mary. The girl was shaking so violently it looked like she was having a seizure, but she was still holding onto her pistol. "Mary, put the gun down." The girl's wild eyes met hers and she nodded, "Please, Mary. It's over."

Mary looked at Bruno and his two companions and her last bit of sanity kicked in. She set the gun on the table and raised her hands in the air. One of the goons moved to grab it, while the other kept his gun pointed at the girl. The man handed Mary's gun to Bruno who stuck it in his chest pocket.

"So, Susan. I can't believe they let you keep your first name. Normally WITSEC makes you change everything. But I guess Susan is so common they figured it wasn't a big deal." The goons laughed like it was a funny joke, but Bruno's eyes were hard and cold, and Susan felt her skin crawl as the man moved closer.

Her heart was pounding so hard she was sure it was going to jump out of her chest, and she felt like she couldn't catch her breath. She didn't dare look at Reed. She loved him and she knew if Bruno figured it out, he'd hurt Reed just to get to her.

"How did you find me?" Her voice sounded more confident than she felt, and she saw something like admiration in Bruno's eyes. The man he'd killed had been sniveling and begging for his life. Bruno had told him he hated cowards just before he murdered him.

"Well you have this little girly to thank for that." He chuckled and gestured at Mary. "I had people monitoring social media using facial recognition software and they came across your crazy little crush here."

Susan felt sick. She'd never noticed Mary taking pictures and she'd been unaware of her obsession. But she should have been paying attention. This was all her fault and she couldn't let Reed and Mary pay the price for her negligence.

"Let them go, Bruno. They don't have anything to do with this. It's me you want. Just let them go," she pleaded.

"Well, that was my intention before we arrived and found this delightful tableau. Now, I'm not so sure. I think I'm going to use this situation to my advantage. Just like I use *everything* to my advantage." The two goons chuckled and nodded.

"What do you mean?" Susan was frantically trying to figure a way out of this situation, but she was coming up blank. Her stomach was doing flip flops and she prayed she wouldn't lose her dinner. She glanced down at Reed who'd been suspiciously quiet this whole time and his eyes were glazed over, face pale, his expression grim.

"What I mean, my dim bulb, is that the girl already shot your friend here. So, if I use her gun to shoot you, then her, it will look like a murder suicide and all be wrapped up in a nice, tidy bow for the cops. Nobody will ever know I was even here." He laughed as he handed his gun to one of the goons. He pulled Mary's gun out of his pocket and raised the pistol until it was pointed directly at Susan.

"Oh really?" A female voice sounded from behind Bruno and his men. "You might want to rethink that plan."

As Maggie stepped out of the hallway, her rifle aimed at Bruno, the back door burst open and four police officers entered, their rifles pointed at his henchmen.

"I suggest you drop those weapons and get on your knees," Maggie said, her voice sweet as sugar.

Bruno grunted at her. The three placed their weapons on the floor, dropped to their knees and raised their hands above their heads.

Susan looked over at Mary. One of the police officers instructed her to stand up, slowly, and put her hands behind her back. The girl's eyes were wild as she looked to Susan for help, but there was nothing she could do: the girl had made her own bed and would have to face the consequences.

She smiled as the murderer who'd caused all the disruption in her life was led away in handcuffs, but she'd been running on adrenaline for too long. Now the ordeal was over, her knees buckled, and she went down.

REED FADED in and out of consciousness. He was supposed to save Susan, but blood loss made him weak and shaky. Luckily, she'd done just fine on her own. He was so proud of her. He knew it was fear and anger that fueled her but whatever the source, her courage was impressive.

For a few moments, when Bruno was holding the gun on Susan, Reed was afraid he'd never get to tell her how he really felt. When he heard Maggie's voice, he nearly cheered; his partner was going to save them, and he could give in to the darkness threatening to envelope him.

He looked up at Susan. She was facing the door, smiling grimly. He reached out to take her hand but suddenly, she lost all color and fell. He grabbed her arm as she collapsed, pulling her onto his lap. The movement depleted what little strength he had left, and as he blacked out, he was happy, knowing he held her in his arms.

14

REED HEARD MUFFLED VOICES. He tried to open his eyes, but they didn't want to budge. His head was pounding, and his shoulder felt like it was on fire. It was too much, and he felt himself slipping away. Just before he lost consciousness, he heard Susan and Maggie arguing.

"I'm not leaving until Reed's awake and out of danger."

"I understand. I don't want to leave him, either, but we need to get you to a safe house."

"No! I'm not leaving and that's final."

He let go and slid into slumber knowing he could relax: his love was safe, and she was watching over him.

REED SLOWLY REGAINED CONSCIOUSNESS. Loud beeping noises and the smell of antiseptic assaulted his senses. He opened his eyes, squinting at the bright light of a hospital room where a white board on the wall said, "Recovery Room Three." Memories started to surface. Mary had shot him in the shoulder, he'd lost a lot of blood, Maggie had arrived in time, Susan had wound up in his arms.

A soft snore interrupted his musings. Susan was there, sound asleep in a chair next to his bed. He smiled as he watched her sleep, marveling at how vulnerable she looked now, after being brave and strong all day.

Susan snorted, shifted in her seat and woke herself up. She sat up and looked around, still groggy from sleep. Her eyes met his and held. Reed's heart lifted at the love he saw shining in her eyes.

Susan stood up and took his hand in hers. "Hello there Mr. U.S. Marshal, you had me worried."

Reed chuckled, then said in his best marshal voice, "Sorry 'bout that, ma'am." He sighed and shook his head, wincing at the pain. "To be honest, I

don't feel very 'marshal-y' right now. I've got a defi-
nite hitch in my giddy-up." Susan giggled.

"And sleeping beauty awakens." They looked up
to see Maggie standing in the doorway, a big grin on
her face. She walked over to Reed and reached for
his shoulder. Even though she didn't touch him,
Reed flinched, and Maggie laughed. "Gotcha! Sorry
partner, I couldn't resist." She took a step back and
looked him up and down. "I've never seen you in a
hospital bed and I have to admit, it's not a good look."

"Wait a minute, what does that mean?" Reed
frowned, wondering if she was insulting him.

"It means, you big goofball, that I want you back
on your feet and out of here, pronto. Your niece
needs an uncle who can babysit so her parents can
have a much-needed date night," Maggie told him.

It took him a moment, but then it hit him. His
eyes opened wide and he grinned. "You're pregnant?
That's amazing!" He lifted his arms to hug her, but a
burst of blinding pain stopped him. He groaned.
"Sorry Maggie, I'll hug you once I've healed."

Smiling, Maggie replied, "No worries, partner,
we'll celebrate when you're better. Right now, you
need to rest."

She looked over at Susan who had tears in her
eyes and a smile on her face. "Maggie, congratula-

tions! That's so exciting! You already know it's a girl?"

Nodding, she patted her belly. "I guess I'm further along than I thought."

The two women embraced. "I'm so happy for you! Can I throw you a baby shower?"

Maggie's glowing, happy expression disappeared as she stepped back into her U.S. Marshal role. "Your WITSEC identity was blown, Susan. We haven't decided what to do about it, but you'll probably be relocated. For the time being, we're putting you in a safe house. You can't go back to your home."

Susan's face paled, and she nodded. "I know that. I guess I just got caught up in the moment." Her voice trailed off and Reed felt his heart constrict. The fear of losing Susan hurt more than the pain in his shoulder. He swallowed hard and tried to blink away the sudden moisture that filled his eyes.

"What's happening with the case?" His deep voice with its pronounced drawl sounded strained and both women turned to look at him, concern on their faces.

"Are you sure you're up for this discussion?" Maggie looked at him quizzically.

Reed swallowed and nodded, afraid to trust his

voice. Maggie looked over at Susan, who bobbed her head.

"Okay then," Maggie blew out her breath. "We arrested Bruno for witness tampering here in Texas, so he's going away for a long time, regardless of what happens at the trial in New York."

Reed grinned at his partner. "Perfect!" He glanced over at Susan, who looked puzzled, and explained. "In Texas, witness tampering is a third-degree felony. It gets the same sentence as the original charges, whether or not that case results in a guilty verdict. As U. S. Marshals we can charge them for federal crimes or turn them over to state authorities."

"That sounds like bad news for Bruno!" Susan grinned, but her face grew serious when she turned to Maggie. "What about Mary? I still don't understand why she left the rosemary. Or was it from Bruno?"

Maggie looked at her thoughtfully. "When you started working at Sweet Grove Middle School, you were given a list of your students, right?"

Susan looked confused but nodded. "I was, yes."

"And the first day of school you took roll from that list."

"Yes, I did." She paused, remembering. "When I

was in school, I had teachers who'd call me Sue or Suzy and I hated it. I always corrected them and said I wanted to be called by my name, Susan. On the first day of class, I asked each student what they wanted to be called and updated the list so I'd remember."

"Well, you might not recall this, but 'Mary' is not Mary's actual name." Maggie grinned and paused.

Reed couldn't stand it anymore. "Out with it, Maggie!"

"Patience is a virtue, Reed," she said sweetly, earning a glare from him. "Okay, okay, drum roll here. Her first name is actually—wait for it —Rosemary."

Reed heard Susan's gasp of surprise and turned to look at her. He could see her wheels turning as she tried to remember. "Oh, my goodness, that's right. I'd totally forgotten. Her full name is Rosemary Garza."

"Mary felt lost after her mom died. She latched onto you and you became a substitute for her mom. A better, nicer version. According to Mary, she left the bundles of rosemary because it's associated with remembrance and friendship. She wanted you to think of her first thing every morning. The rosemary wasn't there to scare you. At least, not till Reed came along."

Susan frowned, but Reed was getting the picture. "So, she shot her mom for not protecting her from her dad, then she told the police her dad killed her mom. She lost both parents in one fell swoop. Not only that, but she was the one who was responsible. Her mental health must have been very fragile at that point." He paused and took a breath. "So, when she met Miss Sinclair, who was kind to her and gave her things she'd been missing in her life, like attention and encouragement, her fractured mind created a relationship that went beyond teacher/student. She left the bundles of rosemary to remind Susan of their bond?"

Maggie sighed. "It's hard for us to understand what she was thinking, but that's the gist of what she told the psychiatrist, yes. And then you appeared, Reed. She saw you as a threat to the relationship she was building with Miss Sinclair and figured she'd have to get you out of the picture. She wanted to scare you away, but when that didn't work, she planned to shoot you like she shot her mother."

They sat silently for a moment, thinking about what could have happened. Reed thanked the Lord that Bruno had appeared when he did. He was certain Mary would have completed her mission to get rid of him. He'd seen her social media and the obsession she had with Susan. Reasoning wouldn't have changed anything. He hated to admit it, but Jenny was right: Mary was too far gone.

Maggie's phone dinged with a text and she looked at the message. "I've got to take this. Some of us have to work for a living, you know."

ONCE MAGGIE LEFT, Susan looked at Reed. She had to tell him how she felt before they moved her, and she lost him forever. Her throat closed up and tears filled her eyes as the grief hit her.

He got shot because of you and he's in pain. Don't you dare get all blubbery right now. You know how ugly you look when you cry! Susan rolled her eyes at her internal pep talk, but it worked. She wiped her eyes and took a deep breath, ready to tell him she loved him.

Reed was watching her, and her heart raced at the look in his eyes. No matter what happened, she was glad she'd met Reed. It would hurt to lose him, but she'd never regret falling in love with him.

She leaned forward and placed a kiss on his cheek. His eyes went wide, and his cheeks turned pink. "What's that for?" he asked, his deep voice turning her insides to jelly.

"Thank you for protecting me," she whispered. "I'm sorry you got shot."

Reed shook his head. "You saved us all, Susan. You kept your head about you and even through your fear, you stood your ground. I just slumped over and bled a lot." He gave her a big grin, and she had to laugh.

"You did bleed a lot. I might never get the stains out of my chair." She stopped talking as the realization hit her. It wasn't her chair anymore. It wasn't her house anymore. Her lower lip started to tremble. Time was running out. She had to tell him. "Reed, I need to tell you something."

A loud beeping filled the room startling them and making them both jump.

"Looks like it's time to replace your IV bag." A cheerful, gray-haired nurse walked around Susan to check the monitors. "Let me turn off that annoying beeping and I'll be right back with a new bag." She pushed a button to stop the noise, turned and briskly walked out of the room.

Susan looked at Reed who was grinning up at her. "I guess you'll have to hold that thought a little longer."

Susan moved out of the way as the nurse returned to replace the IV fluids. "That seems to be the story of my life, lately."

———

REED'S PHONE RANG. "It's time, Reed. I've sent Santiago and Jones to transport her to the safe house. They should be there any minute now." Maggie's voice sounded strained as she added, "keep it together, partner, I care about her, too." The lump in his throat made it hard to speak, so he just nodded at the phone and disconnected the call.

Susan looked frightened. "What's wrong Reed? Are you okay?"

"That was Maggie." He tried his best to sound calm, but his voice came out shaky. He cleared his throat and tried again. "She's sending two marshals to take you to the safe house until we decide our next move."

He watched the emotions play over her face—panic, anger, acceptance. His heart was in a vice and it took every ounce of willpower not to reach for her.

Susan picked up her purse and held it against her chest as if it were a shield. "Okay, I understand."

Reed wanted to reassure her. He wanted to tell

her he would never abandon her. But the decision was out of his hands and he never made promises he couldn't keep. This was one of the hardest parts of the job. He understood now why they stressed, over and over in training, to remove emotion from the equation, or things could get messy.

Reed was looking at Susan when Santiago entered the room and he saw the flash of panic on her face. She turned and looked at him, silently begging him to let her stay. Reed knew he couldn't let her leave without reassuring her.

"Hey guys, can you give us a minute?" Santiago and Jones looked at each other.

"You've got two minutes, then we're taking her to the safe house." Santiago's expression was solemn, and he looked Reed in the eye.

Reed swallowed and nodded. "Two minutes."

Jones looked at Susan. "We'll wait for you in the hallway, ma'am."

"Thank you." Susan waited until they'd left the room before she turned to Reed. "I don't understand why I can't just stay here with you. They can post a marshal outside the door or something."

Reed shook his head. "It's protocol, Susan. I promise, they're good guys and you'll be safe with them. Look, you've been through the wringer today and so have I. We both need food and rest. I'll sleep easier knowing those two are watching over you." Her defeated expression tore at his heart, so he added, "Don't worry, this isn't the last you'll see of me."

Her eyes searched his, looking for the truth. After a long moment, she nodded. "I'd rather stay here with you, but if you promise I'll get to see you before they move me, I'll go with them and not make too much of a fuss."

"I promise," he whispered. "Go get some rest. I'll talk to you soon."

She smiled and stroked his face. "You need your rest more than I do." She leaned in closer and whispered, "You got shot, you know." He laughed, and she gave him an impish grin.

Jones stuck his head into the room. Their two minutes were up. Susan walked out of the room with her head held high, but Reed's heart was heavy.

His mind was racing. He knew what he had to do, and he'd only have one shot at pitching it to his sergeant. He was so close to having everything he'd ever wanted. He couldn't let her slip away.

15

SUSAN SAT at the tiny table in the kitchen of the one-bedroom apartment they called a safe house. Across the room, one marshal was talking on the phone and the other was playing solitaire on the coffee table.

She took a sip of coffee and made a face. She'd never really cared about coffee until she'd met Reed. In only a few days he'd spoiled her. Now she expected every cup to taste as wonderful as his.

Her stomach growled. This morning Santiago brought her a breakfast sandwich from the fast food place down the block. The bun was stale, the egg was an unnatural fluorescent yellow and the cheese looked like plastic. It hadn't made her mouth water like the muffins and the omelet Reed had cooked for her, so she'd left it laying in its sad paper wrapper.

Susan examined the coffee mug in her hands. "Hang in There" was written in big red letters. She turned the mug around. On the other side was a picture of an orange kitten hanging from a rope. Normally that would make her smile, but today she couldn't work up the energy.

When they'd arrived at the safe house, she'd tried to get some sleep. She couldn't get comfortable on the lumpy mattress and her mind insisted on playing the "if only" game. "If only" she'd remembered Mary's name was Rosemary. "If only" she'd seen the girl was unstable. "If only" she'd noticed her taking pictures and stopped her from posting them. Even as she berated herself, she knew if she'd figured it out sooner, she might never have met Reed.

It had been a rough week with her life being turned upside down again. She had every right to be depressed, but that's not who she was. Sure, she'd been through a lot, but this was her life to live and she refused to play the victim. She was over feeling sorry for herself; she was ready to take action.

She walked over to Santiago. "Have you heard any news? When are you shipping me out?"

He glanced up at Susan, grunted, and looked

down at the cards in front of him. He moved one row of cards onto another row. She crossed her arms over her chest and tapped her foot until he looked up at her and sighed, realizing she wasn't going away without an answer.

"Reed was released from the hospital this morning. He and Maggie are meeting with their sergeant. We should have more information soon."

Susan's heart started racing and her mouth went dry. Something was going to happen soon, and she was scared. She wanted to see Reed and Maggie, but she didn't want to leave. Feeling even more unsettled, she trudged back to the kitchen table and her now cold cup of coffee.

REED WAS ECSTATIC. His sergeant had listened to his idea, asked pertinent questions and seemed to accept Reed's answers. He had signed off on the plan and Reed was on his way to talk with Susan. He was grateful that Maggie offered to drive because he wasn't feeling very focused.

Maggie chuckled. "Breathe, Reed. It'll be okay."

"Do you really think so?"

She shook her head and grinned at him. "Just breathe, okay?"

He took one deep breath, then another. It would be okay; it had to be.

They arrived at the apartment complex and called to tell Jones and Santiago they'd arrived. As they walked up to the door, Maggie placed a hand on Reed's arm. "She's been through a lot, Reed, so keep that in mind. No matter what, it'll all work out."

Jones opened the door and Reed walked in. His eyes scanned the room for Susan, but she wasn't there, and his smile faded.

"She's in the bedroom," Santiago said, his eyes sparkling. "Good luck!"

Reed nodded and grinned, embarrassed that he was so nervous, especially in front of his peers. Maggie patted his good arm, then pushed him towards the bedroom.

———————

SUSAN WAS SITTING on the bed, wondering what was going on. She'd been seated on the sofa next to Jones, watching him play his game, when Santiago got a phone call. He nodded at Jones who instructed Susan to go to the bedroom and stay there until they called her out.

She was getting really tired of people telling her what to do. She didn't care if they were U.S. Marshals or not, it was rude. She'd managed to work herself up into a dander and was ready to spit nails when someone knocked at the door.

"You might as well come in. You're going to whether I give you permission or not." She knew she sounded churlish, but she really didn't care. She turned to the door; her arms crossed in front of her, ready to go off on whoever walked in.

She didn't expect to see Reed, and her anger evaporated as he walked into the room. She wanted to throw her arms around him but was afraid she might hurt him, so she just stared up at him, a silly grin on her face. Reed's eyes were shining, but he looked anxious.

"Are you okay?" She was alarmed by how pale he looked.

"Hey, I need to talk to you for a minute. Can I sit next to you?"

"Of course." She scooted over so there was room for him to sit.

He sat down, wincing in pain. She reached out

and took his hand in hers. "Are you sure you should be out of the hospital?"

"It's going to take a while to heal and I'm in pain, but I was cleared to leave the hospital." He lifted her hand to his lips and kissed it. Now he was facing her, his courage was waning. What if she said no? What if she said yes?

Reed cleared his throat and looked into Susan's eyes. "I need to ask you something."

"Anything." She smiled at him and his fears vanished.

"Ever since I met you, I've been amazed by your strength and your determination. You witnessed a murder, you reported it and agreed to testify. You went into WITSEC and started a new life. Crazy things started happening and you never gave up. You've been incredibly brave through the whole ordeal." He gulped and looked into her eyes. "I've never met anyone like you."

Susan's eyes filled with tears. She hadn't felt brave or strong. She'd just done what she had to do and kept putting one foot in front of the other, trusting that God would lead her where she was meant to go.

"Susan, I don't want to lose you. I tried to fight my feelings since they weren't appropriate, but I just couldn't do it. I knew I cared about you from the moment our eyes met. The thought of you leaving and starting a new life has been tearing me apart."

Susan nodded. "I feel the same way. I finally found the man who makes me feel whole, and now I have to leave him behind. But I want you to know, I don't regret a minute of it. You've shown me what love is and I'll cherish every moment we had together."

Reed's face lit up and he leaned towards her. "I wanted to be sure it was possible before I said anything. I couldn't bear to get your hopes up, or mine for that matter. But I got permission, so I need to ask you something."

Susan was confused, but she nodded. "Go ahead, I'm listening."

He swallowed and took a deep breath. "Susan, will you marry me?"

Her mouth dropped open and she felt like the breath had been knocked out of her. "What?" she asked, certain she hadn't heard him correctly.

He grinned. She was so cute when she was flustered. "I'm asking you to marry me. For real."

"But, how? I'm in WITSEC and you're a marshal? Isn't that illegal or something?"

This time he laughed out loud. "It's frowned

upon, but no, it's not illegal. I spoke with my sergeant and got permission. If he'd said no, I was ready to quit the marshals, but he said yes so I can marry you and still keep my job."

Susan's head was spinning. He was willing to quit his job to marry her. Really? *Quit asking questions and say yes*, her inner voice hollered. And this time she listened. "Yes, Reed, yes! I'll marry you!"

Reed's face lit up and he placed a soft kiss on her lips. He'd never tasted anything so sweet. He sat back and looked at the beautiful woman who'd agreed to be his wife.

A cough sounded at the door and a bright-eyed Maggie filled the doorway. "Sorry, but I couldn't wait any longer. Well?" she asked, looking from face to face.

"She said yes," Reed drawled, grinning from ear to ear.

Maggie let out a whoop of joy. "I'm so excited. Now I'm not losing a witness; I'm gaining another babysitter!" She gently hugged Reed, careful not to hurt his shoulder, then gave Susan a big bear hug. "Welcome to the family," she exclaimed.

"I almost forgot. I have good news about your job, too." Susan looked Reed expectantly. "Since Bruno is going away and you won't need to testify, the federal judge decided you don't have to stay in WITSEC. If you want to, you can go back to Sweet Grove Middle School."

"Really? That would be amazing," Susan said. "Of course, I want to!"

"I'm glad because I really want to be there for Tyler and help him finish his origami rose. I promised him I would, and I always keep my promises."

"How are we going to explain everything's that happened? Won't people wonder about me marrying my 'brother'? What about my house? Where are we going to live? Oh, my goodness, there's so much to consider. Do you have a house? Are we going to live there?" Susan's head was spinning, but Reed looked her in the eye.

"All that matters is that you said yes," he told her, and she knew she'd finally come home.

Santiago and Jones came in and while they were congratulating Reed, Susan closed her eyes and said a quick prayer. "Thank You, Lord, for showing me what true love looks like and for keeping us all safe. Amen."

What's our Sweet Promise? It's to deliver the heart-warming, entertaining, clean, and wholesome reads you love with every single book.

From contemporary to historical romances to suspense and even cozy mysteries, all of our books are guaranteed to put a song in your heart and a smile on your face. That's our promise to you, and we can't wait to deliver upon it...

We release one new book per week, which means the flow of sweet, relatable reads coming your way never ends. Make sure to save some space on your eReader!

Check out our books in Kindle Unlimited at
sweetpromisepress.com/Unlimited

Download our free app to keep up with the latest releases and unlock cool bonus content at sweetpromisepress.com/App

Join our reader discussion group, meet our authors, and make new friends at sweetpromisepress.com/Group

Sign up for our weekly newsletter at sweetpromisepress.com/Subscribe

And don't forget to like us on Facebook at sweetpromisepress.com/FB

ABOUT THE AUTHOR

Michelle Francik has always loved to read and write fiction. When she couldn't sleep, she'd create stories and characters in her mind. For a long time, they stayed there. Now that her two sons are grown, she's taking time to do what she loves--write stories that connect with her readers, making them laugh and cry, swoon and sigh.

She lives in South Lake Tahoe, surrounded by mountains, trees, and bears.. She loves the sparkle of fresh snow in the early morning sunlight and the smell of rain, dripping off of the pine trees. She loves to go for drives and find new places to explore that are off the beaten path. She lives with her younger son and his cat, Oreo, and when it isn't snowing, enjoys visits from her older son.

CPSIA information can be obtained
at www.ICGtesting.com
Printed in the USA
LVHW091041140920
665948LV00002B/414